THE EXTRAORDINARY LIFE AND TIMES

OF HENRY WATSON

The Boy from the Future Who Helped Churchill Win the War

R. A. Boyle

First published in Great Britain 2021

Written by:

R. A. Boyle

Published by:

Sue Cameron

Edited by:

Carole Boyle

Sue Cameron

Marc Baker

Cover design by:

R. A. Boyle

Josh Baker

Marc Baker

Special thanks to:

Noah and Dre for their starring roles on the front cover ☺

Martin Taylor and the Hull History Centre for their kind permission to use the original wartime photograph of Bean Street, Hull.

CHAPTER ONE

Henry Watson lived with his Aunt Madeleine, in the market town of Reading. She wasn't his real aunt but had adopted Henry as a toddler. Both of his parents, along with Madeleine's husband, had sadly died in a motoring accident.

Madeleine was born in Normandy and had come to England to take a teaching position at a girls' school in Berkshire. Henry had learned to speak French from an early age, and because it was the only language spoken in their house, he was quite fluent by the time he was ten. Henry was a likeable boy with a winning smile and he attended Hillside Primary School. His school reports showed that he was doing OK at school. He was pretty average at most subjects but he excelled at three; History; French and PE. He was captain of the school football team, and he also played for Berkshire Schoolboys. His ability to mesmerise seasoned defenders with his dribbling skills, and score goals with either foot, meant that his was one of the first names on any team-sheet. Henry also possessed what can only be described as an extraordinary knowledge of British history; Kings, Queens, dates, places, you name it, Henry seemed to know all about it. His history teacher was amazed.

Henry was really looking forward to the school trip planned for the next week, to visit the battlefields and D-Day landing beaches in Normandy. But that was not until Monday. Today was Saturday and Aunt Maddie, as Henry called her, was going to see her old friend who lived in Highworth.

'It's near Swindon,' she told Henry. 'It's very old and full of history,' so he went along for the ride.

'You are driving too fast again,' said Henry, as Madeleine sped along the M4 in her Mini Cooper.

'No, I'm just keeping up with the traffic,' said Madeleine. 'Don't worry so. Anyway, we're nearly there now,' as she pulled on to the slip road at Junction Fifteen and took the A419 to Cirencester. A few miles later, she took the turn for Highworth and within ten minutes they were pulling up outside Maddie's friend's house, who was standing at the front door, waiting to greet them.

'How are you Sally? You're looking well.'

'So are you!' she exclaimed. 'This must be Henry. My, hasn't he grown' and she held her arms out, as if to give him a hug.

Henry was prepared for a handshake but he took the hug anyway (a bit embarrassing for an eleven year old). They went into the house and Sally introduced them both to her Father,

'This is Madeleine, Maddie this is Joe, and Dad, this is Henry'

Henry stuck out his hand very quickly and Joe took it with a smile, saying;

'So, you are the history buff eh? When we've had our coffee, I'll take you out and show you our little town, if you'd like.'

'Yes I would,' agreed Henry.

After coffee, Joe and Henry walked to the end of the lane and turned left at the church, stopping at the sign that read;

WELCOME TO THE 13TH CENTURY MARKET TOWN OF HIGHWORTH

'Wow that's old,' said Henry.

'Yes it is,' said Joe, 'But look at this,' and he pointed out another plaque on the old flint-stone wall:

PERMISSION TO HOLD A STREET MARKET IN THIS SQUARE WAS GRANTED BY KING JOHN IN 1015.

'Now, I know you are into WW2 history Henry. So, come with me.'

They walked a little way to the top of the High Street and Joe stopped.

'Do you see that flower shop over there?' he said, pointing across the road.

'Yes' said Henry.

'Well now, during the war it was the Post Office, showing Henry the plaque on the wall.'

It read:

HIGHWORTH TOWN POST OFFICE

MABLE STRANKS POST MISTRESS

Joe told Henry that during the war, Sir Winston Churchill deemed it highly important that specially selected young men should be trained as saboteurs. In the event that our country was overrun by the Nazis, these men were to be trained in complete secrecy. Consequently, training and spy schools were set up all over the country, in the most unlikely of locations.

'Ours here in the west, was Coleshill House. It was a couple of miles away, sadly not there anymore.'

'Why, what happened to it?' asked Henry.

'It mysteriously burned down, soon after the war. Taking with it all its secrets and any evidence of what went on there. Anyway, let's get back to our Post Mistress Mable Stranks. It seems that young men who had been selected for training for this secret Auxiliary force were sent to this post office with a pre-arranged line of patter like *'Can I buy three one-penny stamps and one halfpenny one please'*, and then pay with half a crown. Whereupon Mable would say *'Just one moment sir, I'll have to go out the back to get your change.'* When the man left the shop, he was met outside by a driver of a truck who asked him to climb in the back and sit down, hidden from view by the canvas flap. He was then taken for a long ride out in the country for many miles, before arriving back at Coleshill House which was less than two miles from the Post Office. In short, he had no idea where he was. Mable Stranks vetted over three thousand Auxiliaries before sending them to Coleshill, and amazingly all in secret. Even her husband didn't know.'

'Wow,' said Henry. 'That's cool, but how do you know all this stuff?'

'Well,' said Joe. 'Shortly after the war was over, Coleshill House burned down and there was nothing left but rubble, no trace at all of what had been going on there, nor any records. But in later years, wartime secrets were released, and many articles were published in the local press. It came to light that when those young men that the Post Mistress had vetted reached the big house, they discovered they were not going to be living in the house, but underneath it in what amounted to a self-contained underground school with classrooms; toilets; kitchens; and sleeping quarters. In the grounds and gardens of the house, cunningly concealed among the shrubs; bushes; and garden sheds, were chimneys; vents; and escape routes.'

'Really?' said Henry. He was finding the whole thing enthralling. 'And what sort of training did they do?'

'They were taught to use explosives; how and where to blow up bridges; map reading; Morse code; first aid; and how to kill a sentry with a knife or a cheese-wire garrotte.' Henry winced and gave a shudder. 'Yeah, sounds awful now, doesn't it? But you must remember, in those days we were talking about the enemy, and the only good German was a dead one.'

'Were you in the army during the war?' asked Henry.

'No, I was at school. I was too young.'

'Where did you go to school, near here?'

'No' Joe replied. 'In the war we lived in Reading. I went to Katesgrove School for Boys'

'Really?'

'Yeah it's kind of hard to explain to you what it was like in those days.'

'Not good then Joe?'

'Well, yes and no. By the way, I think they had one of these training schools in Reading, not sure though, you'll have to google it or whatever it is you younger people do now.'

It had started to rain a little, so Joe and Henry began to wander home, chatting as they went.

'Did you say you were off to France in a week or so?'

'Yes, that's right.' said Henry.

'And will you be seeing the beaches of the D day landings?'

'Yes I think so,' answered Henry. 'Why do you ask?'

'Well,' said Joe. 'If you go down to the seafront, you will see a plaque on the sea wall that reads;

'As you sit here and look out to sea, give a thought for those brave men of many nations who came to save us and free us from the might of the German army. Thousands of these brave men came, many gave their lives that we may be free. Perhaps you may be tempted to say a prayer for them at this time.'

As they walked home in the rain, Henry thought he could see a tear in Joe's eye, indeed he had to confess he felt a lump in his throat himself.

When they got back to Joe's house, Aunt Maddie said;

'Did you enjoy your little tour of the town Henry?'

'Yeah, it was really cool. I had no idea we had trained men to do all that stuff here in our country. Just like the Resistance, in France.'

'That's right,' chipped in Joe. 'And I have to tell you that our Home Guard was not really like Dad's Army, although they did start off like it. But, after a while, they were well drilled and would have given a good account of themselves, Britain's last hope.'

.

CHAPTER TWO

Back in Reading; on the eve of the last day of school before the summer holiday. Henry, along with two of his friends, was playing football. Not a match, just a kick-about in a playing field quite near to where they all lived. All three had changed into their football kit. Henry sported a red shirt with Rooney on the back, and they had stuffed their school uniforms into their school bags. The kick-about was going well, all three boys doing step-overs and overhead kicks and all manner of fancy routines, when quite suddenly it became very dark.

'Looks like rain' said one of the boys.

'No, we'll be alright,' observed Henry. But the sudden flash of lightning and enormous clap of thunder, both coming together, and the rain (the likes of which the boys had never seen) made them change their minds.

'RUN!' someone shouted, and they all three raced across the grass as fast as their legs could carry them. The lightning, striking the ground and scorching the grass, seemed to be all around them. They raced towards the pavilion, just a few yards to go now, but Henry had stopped. He stood there panting and trying to get his breath.

'Come on, Henry!' Shouted the other two.

'No, I left my bag. I have to go back.'

With that, he turned and ran back into the eye of the storm. When Henry reached his bag, it seemed to him he was in a large dry circle, but all around him in every direction was a raging storm. He picked up his bag and was wondering which way to run when he discovered that he had no choice in the matter, because his feet were no longer on the ground and he felt as though he was being lifted. He was in fact, leaving planet earth. The lifting sensation was still with him as he blacked out.

When he came round, Henry found himself lying on a stretcher, mounted on the top of a vehicle of some sort. As far as he could tell, there were no wheels and no driver. Nonetheless, he was being carried along at breakneck-speed through what seemed to be a never-ending tunnel. On and on he zoomed until at last, it seemed to him that he was slowing down. It was then he realised it was not a tunnel, but a passageway he was travelling in. The walls of the passage were metal, which looked to Henry like gold, he was aware that he had stopped moving and was now swivelling to his right, facing a wall of gold. He had expected a door or an opening but there was none. Then, just as if he was watching a cartoon film, a red panel seemed to appear on the wall. It was about the size of a garage door, and to his amazement, he watched the red panel slide to the left, revealing a room beyond. Henry glided-in, and noticed that the gold walls and ceiling of the passage had been replaced with surroundings of white, pure white. In front of him, near his feet, he could see what he assumed was a desk. That too was white, so it was very hard to make out exactly what shape it was. Now he thought he could hear music, not really music as such, but the noise of stringed instruments being plucked, seemingly at random. He could make out the strings of a harp and now, yes, he thought, a banjo and a third was unmistakable, it had to be a guitar. He could hear one instrument at a time. Not a tune, not a chord, just single strings; pluck-pluck-ping. Then a second instrument would chime-in, sometimes two or three at once. It was like listening to a trio tuning up for a gig. Suddenly Henry realised he was not alone in the room; he had been joined by three beings. They looked a little like humans, all dressed alike, in long white hooded gowns, half covering their faces. Their gowns and hair were pure white, but their skin was golden brown. Two of them looked to be male the other seemed more female, somehow. The taller of the two males, who seemed to be in charge, turned to the female being and communicated with her. As his lips moved, Henry heard the sounds of guitar strings and she seemed to answer with the sound of a harp, so he took a guess that the other male would be a banjo. Just then, the female came towards Henry and turned him around to face a blank wall. As he was beginning to wonder what the reason was for this manoeuvre, a large screen appeared on the wall in front of him and although the screen (like everything else) was white, the words scrolling down from top to bottom were black. As he watched the screen and listened to the musical conversation, he realised he was watching an alphabetical scroll of languages, which stopped when English reached the middle of the screen.

'So, you have selected English, Earth boy.' Said the one Henry assumed was in charge. 'Welcome to Space Lab 7.' His voice was soft and calming, no more music now. 'Do not be afraid, we mean you no harm, would you like to know why you are here?'

'Well yes, I would, and I'd like to know WHERE I am as well.'

'You are in Space Lab 7,' came the reply.

'Are we in a spaceship?' asked Henry. Surprising himself that he was curious, rather than frightened.

'Well, not exactly. You see, we are only a small mobile operating theatre. Our mother ship awaits our return when we have completed our mission. At the moment, we have many earthlings to process, and you are one of them.'

'Process?' said Henry. Wondering now if he should be feeling frightened.

'Yes, you see there is a deficiency of Xizodian amongst the people of our planet. Earthlings like yourself possess this substance in their brains and the best age for harvesting is between nine and thirteen years. That is why you are here. Now, if you will excuse me, I must go and get ready for your operation.'

'But!' Protested Henry.

'Do not concern yourself, you will feel no pain and now my two assistants will help you get prepared for the donation. They will answer any more questions you may have.'

Henry had plenty of questions, his first being,

'If you take all of my Xizodian or whatever you said it was, out of my brain, what will I do without it?'

'You don't need it to live on planet Earth, and you won't be moving to our world for another six million years' said the other male.

'Why have I got it then, if I don't need it?' Henry asked, and the answer came from the female,

'You have other things you don't need too, like your tonsils, and your appendix.' She said, pushing him up in to a sitting position. 'Now I need you to be still and quiet, no more questions, please.'

'All ready, here sir.' The second male called to his superior.

'Very good, number one. Let's get started.' He said, as he walked over and stood behind a control panel. His second-in-command took a small handset from his pocket and pressed a button, then looked up to watch a transparent tube, about seven inches in diameter, slowly descending above Henry's head. It inched further down, until it was six inches away and was stopped by the button on the handset.

'All set for green, sir.' Called out number one.

'Then let's go green.' Said the boss, as he flicked a switch on his control panel and watched as the end of the tube above Henry's head, began to glow with a green light.

'OK, you may lower again.' The tube began to slowly descend and was stopped when the green light was just over the boy's forehead.

'Ready for amber, sir.' The man at the controls changed the light to amber and after checking the instrument panel announced,

'Spot on, we will go red.'

He watched as the amber light that looked like a halo around Henry's head turned red and a slight buzzing sound was heard. After about five seconds, the red light changed back to green.

'You may lift now please number one.'

The tube began to rise and as it did so it took with it the top of Henry's head, exposing his brain. With a small silver instrument, similar to tweezers, a minute particle resembling a ripe apple pip was removed from the front of his brain. This was then put into a small container of dry ice.

'Operation complete sir, and the Xizodian looks first class.'

'Well done number one. Now, ready for completion.'

With that, the tube came back down again and Henry, who had felt nothing during the operation, had the section of skull seamlessly placed back on his head. Everything was back to normal, with no visible sign that anything had changed.

The female assistant, who had been holding Henry's hand all the time, said,

'How do you feel earthling? We have finished and can return you now.'

The second in command said;

'But we can't send him back yet, he will be too early.'

'How much too early?' The boss asked.

Having consulted another panel, the operator said,

'It will be about 70 Earth years.'

'That won't be much of a problem, we did it before with that Shakespeare fellow and Newton. It didn't do them any harm.'

The decision having been made; Henry was dispatched back out into the passageway.

CHAPTER THREE

Henry woke up with a thumping headache, sitting on the grass verge of a wide avenue, right next to a bus stop. There was no traffic at all, not even a parked car. He had no idea where he was, or the time of day, but it seemed to be very early in the morning. A nice morning, but fresh, and he felt chilly in his football strip. He looked in his bag and found his school clothes, he changed his shoes and put his trousers and jumper on, then sat for a while wondering what he was going to do. He heard a noise, something was approaching. As it came closer he could see it was a horse and cart. It was a big cart and was full to overflowing with all sorts of junk; an old mattress; bits of metal; a gas stove; coils of wire; and goodness knows what else. It all looked very heavy for the poor old horse to pull, but he seemed content enough as he plodded along. The rather scruffy looking man sitting on top holding the reins was quite small, he was wearing an old black top coat, wellington boots and an old cloth cap. He had a dirty white silk scarf tied in a knot around his neck too.

'Woah, woah' the man cried, and the clip-clop sound of the hoofs stopped. 'Wan' a lift?' The man called. 'You ain't gunner git a bus at this time of the morning, come on son climb up 'ere,' he patted the seat beside him.

Not knowing what else he was going to do, Henry climbed aboard and sat beside the driver.

'Git up, Samson,' said the driver. And slowly, they moved off with a clip-clop, clip-clop. 'What's yer name, son.' Asked the man.

'I don't know,' Henry said, and the driver, who was a little bit deaf, thought he said his name was Joe.

'Well, Joe. His name is Samson, and I'm Fred the rag-n-bone man. Tell me, where are you going?'

'Don't know what to do' Henry mumbled.

The rag-and-bone man thought he said Waterloo.

'I ain't going that far. But I can drop you off on the bus route, if you like.'

They plodded on through the empty streets in silence, Henry pondering his fate. 'Who am I, where am I going?' He thought.

'Are you hungry?' asked the man. Henry, who had been miles away thinking about his problems, was startled by the question.

'Yes, I think I am.' He said, and watched as the man took a huge sandwich from a brown paper bag.

'Do you like bread and cheese?' He asked, as he handed Henry a large chunk of it.

Henry didn't know if he liked bread and cheese or not but, because he didn't want to keep saying 'I don't know,' he just took it and ate it. Thankfully, he discovered that he did like bread and cheese.

'Running away, are we?' Fred asked.

Henry shook his head; he didn't trust himself to speak.

'Don't worry, I ran away meself when I was your age. Look at me now, got me own business and everything. You got any money? 'Ere take this tanner.' He said, as he gave Henry a silver sixpence. 'I gotta turn off up 'ere, but that's your bus stop, just there on the corner. It's a number nine you want, takes you all the way to the station.' He took a pocket watch out of his waistcoat pocket and said, 'Should be along in about five or ten minutes. You won't have long to wait.'

Henry thanked him as he jumped down from the cart.

'Ere don't forget your bag.' Said Fred, as he threw it down to Henry. 'Good luck. mate.' He said, followed by, 'Gid-up!' as he flicked the reins on to Samson's backside. With the now familiar clip-clop clip-clop, they turned the corner and were soon out of sight. Henry walked to the bus stop and from around the corner he heard the cry,

'RAG O BONE. Any RAG O BONE.'

After a few minutes, a red double-decker bus came along. At the rear of the bus was a platform where passengers got on and off. It had a pole in the middle to hang on to.

'Hold tight!' Called the Conductress, and the bus moved forward. 'Where to Deary?' She asked. 'Station?' Henry nodded. 'Threepence please.'

Henry gave her his sixpence and she gave him back three large pennies, and a small green ticket that she had punched a little hole in. He took his change and ticket, and climbed the stairs to the top deck. He sat down behind the only other person on the top deck, and looked again at the three coins he had in his hand. They had Britannia on one side and Queen Victoria on the other. 'Whatever is going on?' He thought. He sat in silence, staring out of the window and trying to make some sense of what was happening to him and why he didn't know who he was or where he was going, let alone where he had come from. Just then, the man sitting in front of him lit up a cigarette. Henry didn't know why but thought to himself, 'He shouldn't do that'. His train of thought was suddenly interrupted when he noticed the headline on the paper the man was reading;

'EVACUATION!'

Worse still, the date on the paper read AUGUST 1st 1939.

'Station, everybody off!' said the Conductress.

The bus stopped right outside the station. Henry took his bag and got off and found that it was raining, so he dashed into the ticket office for shelter. Once inside and out of the rain, he could see a very large group of people, mostly children, making a great deal of noise. Moving forward to have a closer look at what was going on, he noticed on the floor a large green label with a string attached. Out of curiosity, he picked it up to read it. At that moment, a large man with a red face grabbed him by the shoulder and said,

'Oh no you don't, put that label back round your neck and get back on the platform with the rest of your group. Don't try running off again!'

'But...but.' Henry protested 'I'm...'

'Never mind all that backchat, just do as I say, I've had about enough of you lot,' he said. Grabbing Henry by the ear, he pulled him on to the platform, where a train was being loaded with hundreds of children.

CHAPTER FOUR

The steam train standing at the platform was making almost as much noise as the hundreds of young passengers waiting to board. There were about a dozen or so people trying to take charge of the noisy crowd of kids. They consisted of scout masters, ladies from the Women's Institute, and W.V.S. There were other helpers wearing armbands who were now trying to get the children aboard the train. One man, wearing a green armband, said to Henry,

'Right, you look after this lot here,' and he sectioned off a little group of about eight. 'Get on board now and take the first carriage. On you get now, come on let's go, let's go.' Henry didn't seem to have a lot of choice and so with four other younger boys and three girls, he boarded the train and sat down in the first empty compartment. It seemed to take ages to get everyone on board but at last the train appeared to be fully laden and waiting for the off, but before they started the two lady helpers came to their compartment door.

'Right, let's have your names.' Said one of the ladies and read each of the children's number and name from their label. She called it out to the other lady, who wrote it down on her pad. When she read Henry's label, she called out, 'Tommy Barker. No 9462. Age eleven.' Having listed all the names, they went into the next compartment.

'We're going to be here forever,' said one of the boys. But after about forty minutes, the dozens of doors were slammed shut and the shrill whistle from the guard accompanied the huff-and-puff of the engines and great clouds of smoke and steam filled the platform. The train started to move slowly out of the station and a huge cheer could be heard throughout the length of the train. As they moved along the platform, Henry noticed the name of the station was Waterloo, in spite of the fact that all the names had been covered-up with black paint.

'Why have they painted over all the names?' asked one of the girls. Her name tag said her name was Kate. She was answered by a boy near the window who seemed to know the answer to everything.

'It's so that if Hitler invades, he won't know where he is.'

'Well, I hope he doesn't. 'cos if he does, all us boys are going to be carserated.' Said the smallest boy.

'You mean castrated, don't you?' Said another of the boys.

'What's castrated mean?' The little boy said.

'It means they're going to cut off your tentacles.'

'You mean testicles, don't you?'

'Oh yeah,' he said. Henry winced.

'Didn't they give you a lunch box?' Kate asked Henry.

'No,' said Henry. 'I didn't get one.'

'Would you like to share mine? I don't want it all.'

Henry was starving. He had eaten nothing since the rag and bone man's sandwich, and it was now late afternoon.

'Yes please, if you don't want it.' Henry said, and shared Kate's lunch box. Although it was bread and cheese again, it was food. He also drank half the orange juice from the little glass bottle, being very careful not to leave any crumbs in the bottom.

'Where is it we are going to?' Kate asked Henry. He was about to say 'I don't know' when one of the other boys (the one who knew everything) said,

'It's Reading, the place where they make all the biscuits.'

Henry sat silently for a while and tried to gather his thoughts. 'What am I doing here and what is going on? Why don't I know who I am?' The train was slowing down and Henry could make out the name Reading on the blacked-out sign boards as they pulled into the station.

The great steam engine finally stopped, with a huff and a puff. On platform four at Reading station.

'Everybody off,' was the cry. 'All you children with green labels, make your way outside the station and get on one of the Smith coaches with a green label in the front window.

'You there, boy!' Shouted the red-faced Scout Master. 'Take care of some of the younger ones, hurry up now we haven't got all day.' Most of the children had already found the right bus but the young girl with pigtails waited for Henry, and said;

'Can I come with you?'

They sat down together and watched as the line of coaches left the station. Their coach set-off and a few minutes later was pulling-up at the Town Hall. They all got up and made their way to the front when the Scout Master appeared and told the driver that their coach had to go to Katesgrove School instead. They all sat back down and looked out the window as they made their way through the streets of Reading before coming to a halt outside a red-brick school building.

'Make your way inside,' said a lady from the Red Cross, ushering the children into the main hall.

Once inside, they were given tea and biscuits, or cake, or lemonade, or Tizer. Then they were told to find a seat on one of the many folding chairs placed around the hall. Soon everyone had a drink and a piece of cake or biscuits.

Someone at the front of the hall was trying to say something but with the constant babble of all the kids talking at once it was plain he was wasting his time. A shrill whistle from the A.R.P warden brought a sudden hush to the hall.

'That's better,' said the warden, who had volunteered to be a helper for the day.

'Please be quiet now, while Councillor Brown speaks to you.'

'Ahem,' said Councillor Brown. 'Welcome to Reading, all you boys and girls from London. Now, I know you have all had a very long day and we are going to get you billeted just as soon as we possibly can. The Reverend Sanders here,' he indicated the vicar to his right, 'Is the Billeting Officer, and he and his helpers are going to get you all sorted and into your new homes, just as soon as they can.' With that, he turned to his right and said, 'Reverend.'

The vicar stood up and said;

'Now, most of you have already been allocated a Billet. So listen for your names and come to the front when I, or one of my helpers, calls you.'

Henry had noticed a gathering of adults at the front of the hall who were now looking at the very scared bunch of children that stood before them, the adults looked apprehensive too.

'Simon and June Wise,' called out the vicar. 'Come and meet your new carers.' The two children slowly walked forward and met the man and woman they were to spend the rest of the war with. The next name called was Henry's new friend, Kate.

'Wish me luck.' She said, as she walked up to meet her new carer, who was a smartly dressed lady with a nice smile.

'Good luck,' he said.

Henry watched as Kate and her new carer stood and talked and once or twice, they looked over at Henry. The lady went over and spoke to the vicar.

'That young boy there, can we take him to live with us too?' she asked.

'What's his name?' asked the vicar.

'It's Tommy Barker' said Kate, remembering the name on Henry's label.

'No, sorry. He's already been allocated.' Kate and the lady gave Henry a little wave and they were gone. One by one, and sometimes two or even three at a time, children went to the front to meet new carers, but Henry's name had not been called. After nearly all the other boys and girls had gone the vicar came over and said,

'I don't know what's happened to your carer, she should have been here long ago. It's a Mrs Winterbottom, she said she would be here.'

Just at that moment a woman in an overall and bedroom slippers, with her hair curlers covered by a scarf, walked in the door. Henry thought 'I suppose she has come to clean up the hall' but when she came over to the vicar she said,

'I'm Mrs Winterbottom. Is this 'im?' Looking at Henry with one eye, because the smoke from the cigarette dangling from the corner of her mouth was causing the other eye to close. Henry thought to himself 'OMG.'

'We were expecting you here some time ago,' said the vicar.

'Yeah well, I got delayed.' She said.

'Are you still in a position to take the boy?'

'Yeah, long as I gets his ration book and clothing coupons.'

'Oh yes, of course. It will take a few days. But they'll be forwarded on to you'

Turning to Henry, he said.

'Now, you run along with Mrs Winterbottom and she will take you to your new home. As Henry followed her out of the hall, he noticed the thick stockings she was wearing were all wrinkled and nearly falling down. He wasn't looking forward to his new home or to being with Mrs Winterbottom. A short walk from the school and they were in Sherwood Road, there were terraced houses on each side.

'This is it.' She said, when they reached number sixty-two.

There was a little garden in the front of the house. No flowers, but lots of weeds and a rusty old bike with the front wheel missing. She lifted up the letterbox flap and pulled out a piece of string that had the front door key on it. Henry followed the woman into the passage, the house was a typical two up and two down with a sort of annex that was the kitchen and then outside there was a toilet. Gas was connected to the house, but no electric. The gas served the lights downstairs; the cooker; and one gas fire. There were no lights upstairs at all and none in the toilet. You had to take a candle which was not much good on a windy night.

'There's a cup of tea in the pot,' said the woman. 'You can pour yourself one if you like, but I might need something stronger.' There was a cup and a bottle of milk on the table, Henry poured himself a cup of very strong, nearly cold tea.

It was late evening by now and Mrs Winterbottom said;

'While you're waiting for your tea to cool down, I'll show you where you will sleep. We'll do it now, before it gets dark.' In the room at the top of the stairs on the right, which was to be Henry's, there were three things, well four if you counted the window. An iron bed with a lumpy and dirty looking mattress, and an old wooden chest of drawers. Henry put his bag on the floor near the bed.

They both went back downstairs.

'I need to use the toilet please.' Henry told his host.

'Out the back, first door on the right.' She said.

He went out of the kitchen and found the toilet. The inside had once been whitewashed but it must have been a long time ago, because it was peeling off in great chunks now. There was more on the floor than the walls. The toilet itself was a bit like a wooden bench over a basin. Above the bench at ceiling height, was a cistern with what once had been a chain hanging from it. But the chain had long since been replaced by a length of dirty string which if you pulled it several times flushed the toilet. There was no toilet roll but there were some squares of newspaper hooked on to a piece of wire. When he'd finished in the toilet he went back inside and asked,

'Where can I wash my hands?'

'In the sink, of course.' Mrs Winterbottom said, finishing off the last drop of her second gin.

'But there's some plates and stuff in there.'

'Well wash 'em up then boy. I'm not going to keep a dog and bark myself, am I?' she snapped, as she poured another gin.

'Have you got any Fairy Liquid?'

'Any what?'

'Soap, for washing-up.'

'No, use the cocoa tin.' She said, shoving an old tin with several holes punched in the side, and no lid. He had a look inside and saw that there lots of little bits of soap inside. He looked at it long enough to make it clear to Mrs Winterbottom that he had no idea what she expected him to do with it and she snatched it back from him, dunking it in and out of the water until some soap suds formed on the surface. At which point she unceremoniously dumped it down on the countertop and walked out of the kitchen, gin in hand.

Henry got to work and washed the plates and some cups, and had almost finished the drying up when the cup he was holding slipped from his hand and smashed into a hundred pieces on the stone floor. Mrs Winterbottom although nearly asleep sprang up out of her chair and shouted,

'Look what you've done!'

Henry knew what he had done without looking. In any case, what he was looking at was the drunken woman advancing towards him, with a crazed look in her eyes. He thought he ought to run but alas, too late, the swinging blow she aimed at him smashed into his left ear and knocked him to the ground. He got quickly to his feet and ran out of the room, he scrambled up the stairs to his room as fast as his legs would carry him. Once inside the room, he shut the door and found to his relief that the key was in the lock on the inside. He quickly turned the key and locked the door. He stood there trembling for a moment, not knowing what to do next, he went over and sat on the bed, the pain in his ear seemed to be getting worse now that he was able to take time to think about it, and it occurred to him it was the same ear the bully of a scout master had used to drag him onto the platform. No wonder it hurt...

BANG BANG BANG!

'Open this door you little sh**!' He covered his ears with his hands. 'Do you hear me, open this door.'

'I've got to get away from here,' thought Henry. 'But how, with her outside the door? What about the window?' He wondered.

He looked out, it was quite dark now and raining heavily. He opened the window and peered out. The roof of the kitchen was below the window, a drop of about five feet. 'If I can slide down this drainpipe and get onto the sloping roof of the kitchen, I could get down onto the top of that shed and I could jump from there,' he thought. He put his head out of the window and looked at the sloping roof of the kitchen, it looked wet and very slippery 'ooh I don't know, what if I fall??'

He had almost talked himself out of it when he heard,

   'Open the door, you hooligan!'

This was followed by another BANG BANG BANG. Only this time it sounded like she was using a hammer or something similar. His mind was made up, it would be better to risk his life out of the window than have to face that mad woman again. He hesitated no longer, grabbing his bag from the floor, he climbed out through the open window and sat for a moment on the wet sill, it was then he discovered he couldn't reach the drainpipe 'oh well' he thought 'here goes.'

With his bag over one shoulder he turned himself around until he was facing the window. With both hands on the sill and his toes touching the face of the wall below, he began to lower himself down until he was dangling from the windowsill by his hands. His feet however, were still 18 inches above the kitchen roof. He thought about trying to get back up but it was futile, his fingers were beginning to lose their grip on the wet sill and then they slipped right off. Henry dropped onto the sloping kitchen roof with a thud, lying flat on his belly. Now all he had to do was traverse to his left and get down onto the lower roof of the shed. From there he could jump down to the ground, easy-peasy.

Except now, he started to slip. It seemed there was nothing to hold onto and now his feet were almost hanging over the edge. He tried to pull himself up but the slates were too slippery. He noticed however that the end of the roof to his right, just where it joins onto the house, had a strip of lead flashing. Also, the wall itself had one or two nails and things sticking out. He made a grab and got himself a handhold, then got one knee onto the flashing. From there, he was able to climb to the top of the roof and grab onto one of the ridge tiles. Finally, moving to his left, hand-over-hand, he got to the end. He could see the roof of the coal shed, still too high to jump, so he let himself slide down again until he had a short way to jump. Once on the lower roof it was a simple task to reach the ground. The garden was very overgrown but he could see freedom, the garden gate at the end of the path. He started towards it but out of nowhere, arms wide open and feet astride, stood Mrs Winterbottom. Right in his way.

'Gotcha!' She said. Advancing towards him, Henry saw her making a fist.

With his bag under his arm, like a rugby player going for a try, Henry charged past her. Palming her off as he went. He got to the garden gate and looked back to see Mrs Winterbottom, flat on her back in the middle of a large thorny bush. Her legs up in the air, showing her long brown bloomers. Henry ran as fast as his legs would carry him. He didn't know where, he just ran. Down the hill, across a river bridge and then across a railway bridge. He saw a slight hill in front of him, he turned left. A few yards along, he came to Coley Recreation Ground. A sign on the big iron gates said, *'Open from dawn till dusk.'* The gates were open and he went in. Across the grass, at the back of the football pitches, he could see a small wooden building. The door wasn't locked, so he went inside. In the shed, there was a huge pile of nets for the football pitches. Henry laid down on top of them, catching his breath and wondering what to do next. He curled his knees up under his chin in the foetal position and cried himself to sleep.

CHAPTER FIVE

The big Alsatian was licking Henry's face, as though he was trying to bring him back to life. Gradually, he opened his eyes and saw a smartly dressed gentleman leaning over him.

'What are you doing here?' The man asked.

'Nothing sir.' Said Henry, as he started to get up from the pile of netting he had slept on.

'Come, let me help you.' Said the gentleman, offering Henry a gloved hand to help him to his feet. 'My goodness.' he exclaimed. 'You're soaked through, how did you get like that? Were you out in all that rain last night? You had better come with me. Is this your bag? I'll carry it for you. It's not far, just across the road, come along now.' They went out into the sunshine and the big dog followed behind them.

At the edge of the park, and across the road, were some quite large houses.

'He we are. Come in lad' He said, opening the front gate and ushering Henry in.

'Who's that?' Said a fair headed lady, as she stood up from the flowerbed where she'd been cutting some roses for the parlour.

'I don't know yet, Mary. But will you please put the kettle on while I run a nice hot bath? This young man is in need of our help.'

Ten minutes later, Henry was soaking in a hot bath with bubbles up to his neck and smelling of roses, he heard a TAP-TAP-TAP on the door, it was the lady called Mary.

'Would you like me to wash your hair?' She said as she entered.

'No thank you.' Said Henry quickly, which he regretted almost as soon as he'd said it.

'Oh, come now. I'm not going to hurt you.'

'Okay.' He said in a half whisper. Mary knelt by the side of the bath and began to shampoo his hair.

'My-my, it needed a wash.' She said as she gently massaged the suds into his hair. 'What did you say your name was?' She felt the boy tense and he started to sob.

'I don't know. I don't know who I am.'

'Alright, alright. We'll take care of you.' She rinsed his hair with a jug of water then stood up and held up a large white bath towel. 'Out you get, young fellow. Wrap yourself in this. Oh, don't worry. I won't look.'

Henry climbed out and wrapped the towel around him, while Mary dried his hair with another.

'Now then, young man. Tell me what you do remember about yourself.'

Henry didn't answer her. He felt his legs going weak and he dropped to the bathroom floor, in a dead faint.

'George!' Mary yelled to her husband. 'Phone for the doctor quickly, the boy is not well.'

It was some hours later when Henry woke. He found himself in a comfortable bed with clean sheets, in a very cosy bedroom.

'Where am I?' He thought, sitting up and looking around the room. The big dog that had been asleep on the mat made a sort of whining noise, and ran out of the room. In no time at all, he was back. Followed by Mary and George.

'Well, well. How are we now?' Mary asked.

'Where am I, what is happening to me?' Henry said, pleadingly.

'Now-now. All in good time.' Said George. 'You collapsed this morning when you got out of the bath, don't you remember? Early this morning, Shep and I found you asleep in that shed over there.' He was pointing out of the window. When Henry saw the shed and the park, it all started to come back to him.

'Is the dog's name Shep?' He asked.

'Yes, and he seems to have taken a shine to you.' Said Mary, as Shep allowed Henry to stroke his head.

'This is my wife Mary and my name is George. Now who are you?'

A confused look came over Henry's face, and he said,

'I don't know who I am. I can't remember anything except the rag and bone man who gave me a lift, and how I got pushed into being evacuated, when I shouldn't have been. I decided to run away from the awful woman they sent me to, whose house was dirty, and who hit me when I dropped a cup.'

'So that's how you came to be sleeping in the park shed?' Said George. 'But you can't remember anything before the rag and bone man? Well, never mind that for now. Our doctor is a good man and he said you are to get plenty of rest. You've got to take this aspirin with some warm milk and get some more sleep. We will talk again later.'

'Come on, you two.' Mary said to both the dog and George. 'Leave the boy alone to get some rest.'

'Oh. Can Shep stay, please?' Asked Henry. They both looked at each other and Shep seemed to take that as a yes. He padded back into the bedroom and laid down on the mat beside the bed. Henry lay back with his hand on Shep's head and fell fast asleep, not waking again until the next morning.

Shep saw Henry sit up in bed and left the room, scooting downstairs. Two minutes later, he came back with Mary, who smiled when she saw that Henry was awake.

'Good morning, young man. How are you feeling?'

'I think I feel a bit better.'

'Oh good, I'm so glad. Would you like a nice cup of tea?'

'Yes please.' He said, and Mary turned to go, opening the curtains on her way. As she reached the door, she stopped and asked,

'Sugar?'

'Yes, two please.' Henry said, without thinking.

Mary smiled to herself as she went downstairs. 'Well, that's one thing he remembers.' She thought.

George and Mary lived in a nice house on the edge of the park. It was a good neighbourhood and George had a well-paid job, although it was a bit hush-hush. Something to do with M.I.5. Mary didn't know for sure but didn't ask questions. She liked her garden and beautiful rose beds, and kept the front and back lawns neatly trimmed. Tom, the Gardner, came two or three times a week to look after them. They also had an oriental lady called Kim, who would come in part time to help with washing and housework. Mary was talking to Tom in the garden, when Kim brought them out some coffee.

'Ah, thank you Kim. Did you wash the boy's clothes yet?'

'Yes, Missy. Me wash and iron, and sew up hole very good. You see no join. I take up to bedroom now.'

Mary shook her head.

'No-no. I think he's a little too young to be in long trousers. I'll find him something more suitable for a boy of his age.'

Henry was washed and dressed in his new clothes, and was having toast and coffee in the kitchen when George came in.

'Good morning, how are you feeling?'

'I'm okay. Thank you, sir.' Henry replied.

'Call me George. I must say, a good bath, some clean clothes, and a proper rest seem to have done wonders for you.'

Henry looked at his new clothes. He had on a short sleeve shirt; grey flannel short trousers; grey woollen socks held up with elastic garters; and black leather shoes. He had also been given a hand-knitted Fair-isle jumper in green, brown, and yellow.

'But you won't need that yet.' He was told, until the weather cools down.

'Doesn't he look smart, George.' Mary said, as she came into the kitchen.

'Yes, but he could do with a haircut. I'll take him to my barbers next week. Now that you've had some breakfast, would you like to go for a walk in the park? I think Shep will go with you.'

Shep couldn't wait. His ears pricked up when he heard the word park, and he bounded for the door. When the boy and Shep had crossed the road and entered the park, George shut the door and turned to Mary.

'What are we going to do with him?'

'How do you mean exactly?' asked Mary.

'We can't just keep him, he must belong to someone. Where has he come from? Who is he? Who do I report him to?'

'Do you remember when you brought the boy in from the park? You carried his bag in for him.'

'Oh yes, that's right. What about it?'

'Well, it's rather strange really. I asked Kim to wash his clothes and I looked in his bag to see if he had any more washing there.'

'And did he?'

'Yes, he did and he had some other strange things in there too.'

'Other strange things, what do you mean?'

'I discovered nearly all his clothes were made in China, and look at these things (Henry's trainers.) Aren't they the strangest shoes you've ever seen. I have no idea what this small thing with Samsung written on the back could be. There's even a t-shirt with ROONEY on the back, made from material I've never seen before. What's more...'

'There's more?' Interrupted George.

'Yes! Lots more. His name is Henry Watson, he lives at Lower Earley and goes to Hillside Primary School.'

'My goodness,' said George. 'I think you ought to come and work in my department.'

'You're going to need some help from your work people, if you are going to understand this next lot' Mary replied. 'The date in his school books is 2012. In fact, the last date was 27th of July 2012 and that's not all. Look at these.' From her apron pocket she produced a Treasury note proclaiming to be worth 5 pounds, and a silver coin that was stamped 10p on one side, and had a woman's head on the other. Around the edge of the coin were the words '*Elizabeth.II.DG.REG.F.D.2006*'. The same woman's head was on the 5 pound note, wearing a diamond tiara.'

George stared at the strange money and said,

'What's on the reverse side of that note Mary? Wait. No, put it away quickly. The boy's coming back.'

Panting, and out of breath. Henry called out,

'Mary, George. Come quick!'

'What is it?' Asked Mary, as they met in the hallway. 'Are you in trouble?'

'No. I know my name!'

'Good heavens, what is it?'

'It's Henry. Henry Watson. It all came back to me in the park when I heard one of the boys who were playing football, calling to his friend. I thought he was talking to me.' He hesitated a little, and then asked, 'Is this house in Reading?'

Mary and George looked at each other. Mary was about to speak but George held up his hand as if to silence her, and said,

'Why, yes. It's Coley, a part of Reading. Now, do you know what the date is?'

'No.' Henry answered. 'But I know it's late July.'

'What year?' Asked George.

'Well, it's 2012 of course.' Replied Henry.

'Don't you think we ought to have a sit down and talk all of this through?' said Mary. 'Let's go into the kitchen and I'll put the kettle on.'

Soon they were seated around the kitchen table, with a cup of tea and an HP biscuit. Shep was on the mat, beside Henry.

'He seems to want to be with you every moment he can. I just don't understand it. I've not seen him like this before.' George said, shaking his head in disbelief. 'Now then, young man.'

'His name is Henry.' Mary added.

'Oh yes, quite right. I'm sorry Henry. Now, tell me again. What year do you think we are in? 2012 isn't it?.'

Henry nodded.

'Okay, and you come from where?'

'I live in Nutmeg Close, Lower Earley, Reading. Number 23, and our home telephone number is 01189 356541.

'That's not possible.' Mary broke in. 'We don't have numbers like that, our number here is Reading 135.'

'Listen Henry.' said George. 'I'm sorry to have to tell you it is not 2012. It is the year 1939 and you are in Reading, England. We are currently at war with Germany, and you young man, have come here with no ID number; no ration book; and no gas mask. What is going on?'

Henry's face went white, he looked as if he was going to faint.

'I think the boy ought to go and have another lie down George. He doesn't look at all well.'

After a short nap, Henry was drinking the tea Mary had made for him, when George came into the room and said,

'When you finish your tea we are going for a ride in my car, and I want you to show me where you live. Would that be OK, Henry?'

George's car was a fairly new Humber, shiny black and smelling of leather.

'Do you know your way from here to your house?' asked George.

'Well, not from here, no.'

'Okay, where in Reading should we start?'

'Do you know the A329(M)?' asked Henry.

'No, Henry. I'm afraid I don't.' Said George with a very puzzled look on his face.

'Well, you know the M4 motorway...'

'No, I don't know that either.' Said George, looking a bit fed up by now. 'Look, I'll tell you what we'll do. I'll drive us to Earley and you can show me from there.'

George is beginning to think that perhaps Henry comes from another Reading somewhere, or even another world. As they got in the car, Henry was surprised to find there were no seat belts, but he thought it better not to mention it, as George seemed worried enough.

They were driving down Castle Street and Henry noticed the roads were very quiet. In fact, he thought he'd seen more horse-and-carts than cars. However, when they reached the traffic lights at Saint Mary's Butts, there were a lot more cars, and a few odd-looking vans. To his left, he saw a red bus with two long wooden arms reaching up from the roof that connected with overhead electric cables.

'What's that?' he asked. 'It's a trolley bus.' George told him.

'I know where I am!' Henry cried excitedly. 'This is The Butts and you can't go down there.' He said, as George took a right turn in front of the Cross Keys pub. 'It's one way!'

'No, it's alright. This is a two-way street. Always has been.' George replied, reassuringly.

On Bridge Street, they came up behind a pair of enormous Shire horses pulling a Drey, loaded with Simmonds beer barrels. Henry asked what the boy in the uniform was doing, and George explained that the poo-boy was employed by the brewery to pick up all the mess that the horses left, as they did their business in the road, while they walked. '

Mary likes me to bring some home whenever I can, as it's an excellent manure for the roses.'

Soon they were in Southampton Street and strangely, there was no flyover and no IDR. The Oracle shopping centre was nowhere to be seen either.

'I know this road too. My aunt has a friend who lives in a flat, just there.' Henry pointed, as they passed a row of about 6 three-storey buildings.

'Good,' said George. 'Now we are getting somewhere.'

When they got to Whitley pump, they took a left. Not many houses here, but lots of trees. They took another left at a pub called The Merry Maidens.

'Yes, I remember this. But it's changed a bit. It looks different somehow.'

'Where do I go now?' George asked, and added, 'This is Earley.' Henry was puzzled because it all looked different. No houses, or the school where it should be. There were one or two cottages with thatched roofs along the road, but not the housing estate the boy had described, only farmer's fields.

'I'm sorry.' Said George. 'I guess it's just not here. We had better go back.' He could see Henry was upset so said, 'I tell you what we'll do. I want to go back down Southampton Street and buy a lardy cake from the cake shop, then we'll stop and see if we can find your Aunt's friend. Perhaps she can help.'

They stopped the car outside Rose the Bakers, went in and were lucky enough to get the last one. George put the cake in the car and said 'Come on we can walk from here, what number did you say it was?'

'It's 160 Flat C' Henry replied.

'And her name?'

'Colette Leon' said Henry.

'Here we go then.' said George as they stepped up to the front door.

'That wasn't there before.' Henry said, pointing to a brass plaque on the wall which read 'Miss Sumpster - Dressmaker'.

'There should have been four doorbells too,' thought Henry. But there were none. George used the knocker, his RAT-TAT-TAT was followed by silence for what seemed an age but at last the door was opened by a plump middle-aged woman with a red face and fair hair.

'Can I help you, she asked?'

'Yes,' said George. 'We are looking for a lady named Colette Leon who lives in flat C.'

'Oh no my dear you must have the wrong address there are no flats here.' 'Who is it?' called a woman's voice from somewhere inside. 'Someone at the wrong address.' said the red-faced lady, 'Sorry.' and she shut the door. 'It is the right house' said Henry 'Because it is the third one up from the corner' George was feeling sorry for this young boy but was at a loss to know what to do next, he put his arm around his shoulder and said

'Come on let's go home now.'

Later that night George sipped his whiskey and said;

'Mary, I just can't make it out. He seemed to be so sure, he knew some of the things and places we went to today but his house and school were just not there.'

'Yes. I don't know what to make of it all.' there was silence for a while then Mary said 'They wouldn't be, would they?'

'Wouldn't be what?' asked George.

'Don't you see?'

'No, I'm afraid I don't.'

Well, if he has come back from the future, they would not have been built yet.'

'Oh my goodness, I see what you mean.' They sat in silence for a while then George said 'I think I need another drink.' Whilst he was pouring his whiskey he said 'Mary, consider this..... an 11-year-old boy is living in Reading or should I say going to be living in Reading in seventy years' time and somehow, God only knows how, he turns up here now. So, if we try to forget for a moment that the whole thing is just downright impossible, and assume he really is from the future just think what he could tell us about our future.'

'Like what for example?'

'Well like the outcome of this war to start with and lots of other things too.' He was interrupted by a tap

tap tap on the door, Mary opened it and Henry was standing in the hall in his pyjamas.

'Is it alright if I get a drink?' he asked. 'I can't get to sleep.'

'Yes of course it is but now you are up do you think you could answer a few questions?'

'Yes, I will if I can.'

'Good. Come and sit down, can you tell me the name of our Prime Minister?'

'Yes, it's David Cameron.' but the look on George's face told him it was not the answer he wanted. 'Or do you mean for World War 2?'

'No. That's not right I'm afraid. But, did you say World War 2?'

'Yes,' said Henry. 'We've just been doing World War 2 history at school and the Prime Minister was Winston Churchill.'

'Well, you've got that wrong my lad,' Said George. 'The Prime Minister is Neville Chamberlain.' Mary butted in at this point and said,

'The news is just coming on the radio, should we listen to it?' After listening to the chimes of Big Ben (Ten Dongs) a voice said;

'This is the BBC News with Peter Barnes reading it. It was announced tonight that the Prime Minister Neville Chamberlain has resigned and the position has now been accepted by the right honourable Mr Winston Churchill who was sworn in at Buckingham Palace, by his Majesty King George VI, at 5:30 this afternoon. The new Prime Minister will address the nation at 9 AM tomorrow morning. Other news now'

'How on earth did you know that?' Mary asked, her face looked drained and George thought she was going to faint.

'Sit down Mary' he said. Turning to Henry he said 'But how did you know?'

'I learnt it at school, and shall I tell you what he said in his speech?' asked Henry.

'Do you mean to tell me you know what Churchill is going to say in his speech to the nation when he's not going to speak until tomorrow?'

'Err yes. I can't remember everything about it but he said we will fight on the land we will fight on the sea we will fight on the beaches and we will fight on the air, we will never surrender, or something like that it's quite a famous speech.'

George took a large gulp of his whiskey and as he poured himself another, he said;

'I think we had all better go to bed now and see what the morning brings.'

The following morning, all four (including Shep) gathered around the radio and listened to the words of the new Prime Minister, who told the nation of the *'dark clouds of war'* over our country and how we must all be prepared to do our part to defend the nation against the German aggressor and *'we will fight, yes we will fight on the land, we will fight on the sea, we will fight'*..... Mary fainted.

'Quick. Get a glass of water please Henry,' George instructed.

Mary came round quite quickly once George had applied a wet towel to her forehead and had given her a few sips of water.

'How are you feeling now?' he asked.

'OK, I think. George, I must talk with you.' Then, looking at Henry she said, 'Will you please take Shep for a run in the park?' When they had gone she said, 'That boy frightens me George, have you spoken to your friend the Chief Constable yet?'

'No, not yet, there are so many things I want to try and find out about first. Let's hang on for a while, it all seems so unbelievable that he has somehow come from the future. Perhaps, just perhaps, he has. Why don't we wait a little while longer or do you think we should have him locked up or something?'

'Oh, good heavens no,' cried Mary. 'It's just that it's all a little scary and I don't understand why a 10 year old boy would go to school with that amount of money, if indeed it is real money and not imitation money from some game like Monopoly.'

When Henry returned, he could see his bag on the table, and Mary and George waiting for him.

'Now, we would like you to explain these things please,' George said, as he emptied the contents of Henry's sports bag on to the kitchen table. 'Sit down please, and tell us what this is.' He picked up the red shirt,

'It's my Man United football shirt.'

'Why does it have the word Rooney on the back?'

'It's not a word, it's his name.'

'Whose name?' asked George.

'Well, Rooney's of course. He's one of the best players in the world.'

'And he plays for Manchester United?'

'Yes'

'Well, why have you got his shirt?' interrupted Mary.

'Never mind that for now, let's go on to the money.' Said George. 'What's this?' and he held up the five-pound note.

'It's five pounds.'

'And who is this lady?'

'It's the Queen of course, Queen Elizabeth.'

'That would be King George VI's eldest daughter, Princess Elizabeth I suppose?' said Mary.

'Just how long has she been Queen? With the King still alive, I can't quite believe I'm asking this.'

'I don't know,' said Henry. 'But she has just had her diamond jubilee and we all had a day off school.'

The next question surprised Henry.

'Now, how does a boy your age come to be carrying such a large sum of money?'

(£5 in 1939 would be worth about £300 now.)

Henry told him five pounds would buy a happy meal at McDonalds or a banquet for one at KFC or in the supermarket...

'Hold on, hold on, hold on,' said George. 'What is a supermarket, and what are McDonalds or KFC and what on earth is a motorway that you spoke of earlier?'

It was way after midnight when Mary said;

'The world you lived in was clearly way ahead of ours.' Especially when she learned about computers, HD television, mobile telephones, moon landings and so much more that was yet to be invented.

'Let's get back to the war,' said George. 'What can you tell us?'

'What do you want to know?' asked Henry.

'Well, who wins for instance?'

'Oh, we did.'

'Who's we?'

'The Allied Forces of course.'

'Allied Forces??'

'Yes. Britain and America, oh and the Russians.'

'And how long will it, I mean did it, last?'

'I don't know for sure, but I think it was about five years.' They sat there for a while until Mary said,

'Let's all get some sleep now; I'm sure the lad can tell us some more wonders tomorrow.'

The following weeks were full of questions, some of which were too technical for Henry to answer and he was asked to make a list of the things that were different now to what he was used to, so he made the following observations;

- People wear strange clothes
- There are not many cars and most of them look funny
- The milkman has a horse and cart, so does the baker
- There are no televisions, computers, mobiles or iPads
- There are no motorways, jet planes, or supermarkets
- There are no McDonalds or Kentucky Fried Chicken
- There is no electric light in most houses, only gas
- There are no washing machines or fridges etc etc

There was a lot more (most of the above had not been invented in 1939.)

CHAPTER SIX

George just didn't know what to do about Henry, but after consulting with his superiors it had been decided that the boy could stay where he was. He would not be allowed to go to school though. Instead, he was to continue with his education at home. Mary, being an ex-teacher, was asked to volunteer. He was to be able to mix with other boys, but under oath not to talk about his other life, he was just to be another evacuee.

(What a valuable asset to the war effort the Home Office had found.)

School started again on the first Monday of September.

'We are going to have to start right at the beginning with this subject,' Mary said. 'Pounds shillings and pence.' She knew Henry didn't have a clue. On a small blackboard she had hung on the wall, Mary wrote the following words, from top to bottom; farthing; halfpenny; penny; three pence; sixpence; shilling; and half a crown. At the top of the list, she wrote 'pound' and she put her chalk down.

'These are all of our coins, now you must learn their value.' She turned to the blackboard once again and wrote;

- There are 8 half-crowns in 1 pound

- There are two shillings and sixpence in 1 half-crown
- There are 20 shillings in a pound there are 12p in one shilling
- There are 6 pence in a sixpence
- There are 3 pence in a three penny piece
- There are two half pennies in one penny
- There are four farthings in one penny
- There are 240 pence in a pound

'We also have crowns and guineas,' she added. 'But we do not use them anymore. You should know a crown is worth five shillings and a guinea is twenty-one shillings, used only in the tailoring trade and horse-racing world.'

'Now, for our banknotes. Our smallest note is a 10 shilling and next is a pound note. The next is a 5-pound note and that looks like this.' She produced a rather plain looking piece of paper about 10 inches long and four wide and in scrolled black writing it said Five Pounds.

'Not really like a bank note at all' thought Henry.

'Now then, let's see how you get on with the simple sums.'

Lunchtime could not come quick enough and if there was one thing that he learned that day, it was that Maths had just become his least favourite subject. Mary was enjoying herself, as she had always loved teaching and her old classroom skills had never left her. When it came to French, which was taught as the only foreign language in English secondary schools, Mary knew she would be unable to teach him.

'Therefore, we will do Spanish instead' she informed him.'

'Okay,' he said. 'I know a little Spanish.'

'Do you?' she said.

'Si,' said Henry. 'I've been there, on holiday,' and Mary sat dumbfounded listening to this 11-year-old boy talking of the places he had been, including the USA.

'Oh, my goodness,' was her comment. 'Wait until I tell George.'

Life was good for Henry even though there was a war on and he had to do without TV and iPads and computers etc. The food wasn't too good either, but he did have a wonderful friend in Shep. They had become inseparable and when he was asked,

'Would you go back to your old life in 2012 if you could?' Mary asked,

'Only if I can take Shep.'

Something else he enjoyed was telling Mary and George things that were going to happen before they actually did. One evening, for instance, George said to him,

'Walt Disney's new film *The Wizard of Oz* is on at the Vaudeville, shall we all go tomorrow,'

'Oh, I've seen it. I've got it on DVD, and I've got Pinocchio too.'

'You've got it on what?'

'D.V.D. It's a little silver disc, about this round (he made a shape with both hands) and you put it in the player and then watch the film.'

'Watch it where?'

'Oh, you watch it on the television'

'This disc, is it real silver?'

'No of course not, it's made of plastic.'

'What's plastic?'

'Mary, will you come in here and listen to this boy.'

The next day, all three went to see the film, Henry promised not to tell them anything about it.

CHAPTER SEVEN

Henry was talking to George one day about Shep and he asked him,

'Is it normal for an Alsatian to run as fast as Shep?'

'No,' said George, and he told him the story of how they came to rescue Shep. 'Many years ago, I used to breed Alsatians and I won quite a few cups and medals but had to give it up because of my work. Then, about a year ago, the police came to see me and told me about a dog that was running wild, killing rabbits and chickens in order to stay alive and also killed a few cats, which didn't go down very well with the owners. The police informed me they intended to shoot the dog, but they knew I used to be a breeder and asked if I would like to try and save him? So, that afternoon I went with the police along the riverbanks to the fields where he'd been sighted. After about 10 or 15 minutes we saw him, he was as thin as a rake and looked more like a wolf than a dog. *'What do you think?'* asked the marksman. I asked him to stand back and let me approach the dog alone. *'Well, okay. But you must be careful.'* I took the lump of meat out of the bag I was carrying and slowly walked towards him. He made no attempt to run away and took the meat from my hand and started eating it. As he did so, I took the collar from my bag and gently put it around his neck, talking to him all the time. I attached the lead and said, *'Come on boy let's go home.'* The policeman stood back, amazed as we walked past. Mary was a little wary of him at first but after a few short weeks of love and care he looked like a proper dog.'

'Do you think he could win medals in the show?' Henry asked.

'No, I'm afraid not. His tail twists over to the left and he has got a lazy ear. The left one here, you see, is quite floppy. The only time he pricks them up properly is when there is danger. His other problem is he still chases cats.

'Oh no,' said Henry. 'I've stopped him doing that.'

'How?' asked George.

'I told him not to.'

'Well, I'll be darned.'

'It's no wonder he can run so fast.' Henry said, and he told him of the day in the park when two men with a pair of greyhounds were there. 'One man held onto the two dogs by their collars whilst the other walked across the grass about 200 yards away. I had Shep on the lead and we were about 5 yards behind the two greyhounds and then the man two hundred yards away waved the white flag and blew a whistle. The two greyhounds streaked across the park and Shep went too, wrenching the lead out of my hand and amazingly he not only caught up with the two racers but beat them to the flag which she snatched out of the man's hand and brought it back to me. When I gave the man his flag back, I told him I was sorry.'

'What did he say?' asked George.

'He asked me if I wanted to sell the dog.'

'Well bless my soul,' said George. 'What else has he been up to?' Henry told of his latest trick, where he gave the order 'HIDE,' Shep quickly disappeared behind a bush or tree and stayed hidden until the command 'SHOW,' which would see him leap out like a tiger.

'Oh my goodness. Be careful you don't frighten anyone with that trick.'

What Henry didn't tell him was that he already had. It had happened a couple of weeks ago when he had taken Shep across to the park for a run. As they got there, Henry heard a girl scream. He pushed through the bushes, onto the path, and saw two boys bullying a young girl. She had her hair in pigtails and the boys seemed to be having great fun pulling them. Henry looked at Shep and said 'HIDE.' Shep disappeared into the nearest bush. '*Well here goes,*' he thought, as he stepped out onto the path.

'Hey, stop that!' He shouted. Then he noticed how big they both were.

'What's it got to do with you?' snarled one of the boys.

'Just leave her alone that's all,' said Henry.

'Who's going to make me?' said the larger of the two bullies.

Henry gulped and said,

'I will.'

'Yeah, you and who's army?'

'Me and my friend' said Henry'

'You ain't got no friends.' He said, turning to his pal. 'Come on, let's give him a good hiding.' Slowly, they started to come towards Henry, although the pal stayed back a couple of paces.

'You had better not come any closer,' said Henry.

But they kept coming.

'This is your last warning. Stop!'

They grinned at each other, clearly not taking him seriously.

'OK you've asked for it…. SHOW!'

Shep sprang out of the bush with mouth wide open, fangs showing and snarling like a wild tiger. His front paws landed squarely on the boy's chest and knocked him to the ground. Both boys screamed at the same time. The one at the rear went hot-footing-it out of the park but when he reached the gate he could still hear his pal screaming,

'Get him off, get him off!'

'Let him up, Shep.' Said Henry. 'And you.' he said, looking at the white-faced wretch on the grass, 'You go over to that young girl and tell her how sorry you are, and that you won't ever tease her again. Go on, do it now.' To help him on his way, Shep bared his teeth and gave a growl. After the boy had apologised, he left the park making a mental note to never return. In the meantime, the young girl had come over to Henry and said,

'Thank you for helping me, you were ever so brave.'

'That's alright,' said Henry, trying to look calm (although he was still shaking).

Then the girl said,

'I thought your dog was going to kill him.'

'Oh no.' he said. 'I knew he wouldn't do that,' but deep down inside, he had thought so too.

'Haven't I seen you before?' the young girl asked. 'On the number three train?'

'Oh yes,' said Henry. 'Now I remember. Your name is Kate isn't it?'

'That's right,' she said. 'Your name is err,'

'Henry,' he said.

'Oh, is it? I thought it was...'

'No no, it's Henry,' he cut in. Changing the subject, he asked 'How are you getting on in your new home? Is that lady who came to pick you up as nice as she looked?'

'Yes, she is, and do you know what? She is a real lady and we live in a great big house. She is married to Lord Palmer; he is nice too and our house is not very far from here.'

'What about you? Did you get billeted with someone nice?'

'Err, yes I did. Not a Lord and Lady but they are very nice, and I live in that house there.' He pointed to the middle one of the three large properties.

'Really?' she said. 'How odd.'

'What's odd about it?'

Well, the chauffeur dropped me off here in the park and said he was going to see his mother for an hour, and when he comes back, we have to pick up a man from that house and take him to the Grange, that's where we live.'

'What is the man's name?' asked Henry. 'I don't know for sure but I think it might be George or something. I don't really know, as I'm not supposed to hear everything that goes on at the Grange. There seem to have a lot of hush-hush meetings going on, quite spooky sometimes. Oh, look. The car is back so I have to go.' She pointed across the road towards the big black Bentley that had pulled up outside the house where Henry was living. 'I hope we meet again and thanks for saving me from those boys.'

She walked across the road to the car and the driver opened the door for her as if she were royalty. He then walked around and held the other door open for the passenger he'd come to pick up. Henry, for some reason that he didn't understand, decided to stay out of sight behind the bushes and watched as GEORGE got into the car. The driver shut the door, and then took his place behind the wheel of the car, before it sped away.

In the months and years ahead, Kate and Henry would become the best of friends. Weekends and holidays, they spent hours of leisure time together, swimming, cycling and rambling in the Berkshire countryside. They became like brother and sister. Kate came to Coley in a chauffeur driven limousine to take George to work (whatever that was) and Mary became very fond of her. As the months went by, she persuaded Kate to change her hairstyle from plaits to a ponytail. 'Suits you much better' she said and even Shep, who had become her second-best friend, seemed to think so too.

CHAPTER EIGHT

The favourite swimming place for kids was called Monkey Island. It was a couple of miles along the towpath of the River Kennet, a walk that Henry and Kate both enjoyed. Shep who always went with them was wild with excitement whenever they were going swimming. It was fun to chat to the fishermen along the riverbank and enquire about how the fish were biting.

Monkey Island was so named, not because there were monkeys there but because the water from the Holy Brook flowed into the Kennet at that point and formed a large natural pool. In the middle of it was a small stony island and so it was assumed that the Holy Brook, in times gone by, was used in some way by the holy order of monks, From Reading Abbey. Perhaps they came to bathe or to do their washing there years ago. Who knows? Whatever the name, it was a good place to swim. On one side of the river pool was a lock gate which controls the amount of water that flowed into and out of the pool and the riverbank near the lock was about 10 feet above the water, making a perfect place to dive from, it was also the deepest part of the pool. Kate refused to enter the water from this point, and so did Shep. Instead, they went around to the little sandy beach and waded in. Henry took a run and dived in. He hit the water about 10 feet from the bank, it was always best to dive out as far as you could, because the lock gates controlling the flow of water in and out of the basin always cause an undercurrent close to the bank. When Henry had dived-in he felt the undertow was quite strong, much stronger than usual in-fact, perhaps that's why there's a notice saying 'DANGER NO SWIMMING' he wondered.

Two other boys, who were in the water playing with a ball, threw it to Kate and when she threw it back, the other boy threw it to Henry. Shep joined in and they were all having a super time until the ball sailed over Henry's head and on towards the lock. Henry turned and swam after it, but the wind seemed to take it further and further away. Henry was a good swimmer and with a gigantic effort and rush of energy he reached the ball. What he had not realised was just how close he had come to the lock, and the strong pull of the undertow was dragging him down. He swam with all his might, but the current was too strong, he was getting nowhere, and now he could barely keep his head above water.

'HELP' he managed to shout, but Shep was already on the case. With all the speed he possessed, he raced around the side of the lake and when he got to the spot that Henry had first dived in from, he launched himself into the water just in time to see Henry's head disappearing. He grabbed a mouthful of hair on the top of his head and yanked his head above the water. Henry was blue in the face and gasping for breath as his head came out of the water. He splashed and kicked against the strong pull of the underwater current and then his right hand managed to grab Shep's collar and the two of them were able to move away from the pull of the current. For a moment or two though, it seemed even the combined effort of boy and dog would not be enough.

'Come on SWIM!' Shouted Kate.

'SWIM, come on!' Shouted the other two boys.

They all knew it would be senseless to get in the water themselves to try and help,

'SWIM, COME ON!' they shouted, and then oh-so-very-slowly the pull of the current began to ease. A few strokes more and they were free of the current altogether. Kate and the two boys ran back to the little beach and ran into the water to help pull Henry and his dog out onto the shore and safety. They all collapsed except Shep, who first shook himself violently from side to side to remove the water from his coat and then went over to Henry and started to lick his face in much the same fashion as he'd done when they'd first met in the shed in the park.

'I think he likes you' said one of the boys. 'That's the bravest thing I've ever seen, I think that dog deserves a medal' the second boy said.

'So do I' said Kate. 'I sometimes think he was put on this earth just to look after Henry. 'Do you know that dog had to be banned from the park when Henry is playing football?'

'Why is that?' the two boys asked. 'Well, it used to be okay for a kick-about but even then, the dog wanted to join in, and if Henry got fouled, Shep had to be restrained from running onto the pitch and attacking the aggressor. Now that Henry has been picked to play for Coley Boys, Shep has been banned from the park when there is football practice or a game. It's only right because defenders were afraid to tackle Henry, for fear of getting attacked by the dog.'

The boys laughed and Henry said,

'Yes, but he wouldn't really hurt them.'

'Is your name Watson, Henry Watson?' Asked one of the boys. 'You must be the new kid they were talking about, who does all them fancy step-over's and stuff. Oh my God, I play for Whitley Wanderers and we've got you in the semi-final at Prospect Park next week.'

'Yes, I'm looking forward to it.' Henry said. 'May the best team win, cheerio, see you soon.' The boys said goodbye to Henry, Kate and Shep and they got on their bikes and left for home with plenty to tell their mates.

CHAPTER NINE

One morning, Henry looked out of the kitchen window, and to his horror Tom the handyman-cum-gardener had dug up all of Mary's beautiful prize-winning roses.

'Look what Tom has done,' He called out to Mary.

'I know,' said Mary. 'I can barely bring myself to look. It's awful isn't it? But we must all do our bit. It's called *Dig for Victory*. So instead of flowers we must all grow vegetables. Tom is going to plant potatoes, cabbages, beans, and lots of other veg. It's very important. You see, Britain doesn't produce enough to feed us all, we rely on imports from other countries and the merchant ships bringing us food are being sunk at an alarming rate. In fact more are being sunk than are reaching our shores. Hitler thinks that when we are all starving, Britain will surrender.'

'How are the Germans sinking all our ships?' asked Henry.

'It's all done by those sneaky U-boats,' Mary replied.

'U-boats, what are they?'

'Submarines, out in the north Atlantic. They seem to be able to torpedo ships and then run back to their base with ease.'

Henry thought for a while and then said,

'I think I remember the RAF being very successful in bombing all their bases, which stops them getting out again, but I don't know when.'

'I just hope it's soon, we can't go on like this for much longer,' Mary said with a sigh, before asking 'Do you like turnips?'

'I don't know what they are,' Henry replied.

'Oh dear, what about swedes?'

Henry looked puzzled,

'I don't know much about them; I've never been to Sweden.'

'What ever did they feed you in your future world?' Mary said with a smile, remembering to tell George this little gem.

'Why don't we keep some chickens?' asked Henry. 'Then we could have lots of eggs.'

Yes, George is okay with that, but he refused to even think about us having a pig in the garden. But veg and chickens are okay, he agreed last night that we all have to do our bit.'

(Henry too was to do his bit, but in a different fashion.)

One evening, George said,

'Mary, do we still have any of that nice Sherry left?'

'Yes,' she replied. 'I left it in the kitchen.'

'Have you been taking a crafty nip with your afternoon tea?' He asked, jokingly.

'No of course not, she replied. I used it in the trifle I made for Sunday tea. Why do you want sherry? Who's coming?' She asked, knowing that George only drank scotch.

'It's Reggie Mitchell, you remember him? He is the aircraft design chap we met last month at Portsmouth. He is going to drop in this evening on his way down to the south coast somewhere.'

'Oh yes, I remember him. Nice man, very quiet.'

'Yes, that will be him now,' said George, when he heard the doorbell ring.

'Hello, Reggie old chap. How are you? Do come in, we will talk in my study.'

'That will be fine,' Reggie replied. 'I won't keep you long, I just wanted to update you on the K5 project.'

'Oh yes, how are we doing on that one?'

'We are doing rather well, it's ready to go into production, should start next week.'

'Well, that is good news.' said George. 'Would you like a drink?'

Just at that moment, Mary came in with the sherry.

'What wonderful hosts you are.' Said Reggie. 'To remember my favourite tipple.' George poured drinks but Mary declined and said she had things to do in the kitchen. 'A woman's work is never done' said Reggie, and Mary left the two men to talk in peace.

'Well now that is good news about K5, but tell me how is the upgrading of your Supermarine going?'

'Slowly, I'm afraid. We have a meeting on the south coast tomorrow and we are hoping the boys have come up with new ideas, because our current fighter planes are just not up to it. The Luftwaffe have some mighty-fast machines and we need something better, and quickly.'

'Well, I do hope you can come up with something soon for all our sakes,' said George.

'We are doing all we can,' said Reggie. 'Let's just hope it's enough. I must go now; I want to make the coast before dark. The tiny little slits they have left on my headlights are no more illuminating than a candle.'

Henry was in the hallway, playing with the model aeroplane he had just finished making. He held it aloft in his right hand and had the little plane diving and dropping sideways and swooping in a tight loop as though following a German fighter plane. George and his guest walked out into the hallway, and when Reggie saw the sweeps and dives Henry's plane was making, he asked,

'What kind of plane do you call that?'

'It's a Spitfire,' Henry replied. He had carved it out of balsa-wood and from memory he thought it looked like the famous World War II Spitfire.

'I wish I could get my planes to manoeuvre like that,' Reggie said with a sigh.

'You should watch the birds sir.' said Henry.

'Watch the birds you say, well maybe I will. Goodbye George, must dash.' He called goodbye to Mary and was gone. George looked at Henry's little plane and said,

'Where did you get the name Spitfire from?'

'That's what it's called, or that's what it is going to be called.'

'Is it going to be very good?' George asked.

'Yes, the best. It will outfly and out-manoeuvre anything the Germans have. In fact, it will win us the Battle of Britain.'

'What is the Battle of Britain?' George asked.

'It's the battle for the skies' said Henry.

'Why did you not tell us this before?'

'You didn't ask me, and anyway it's going to happen whether I tell you or not. Because it already did.'

Reginald Mitchell, the aircraft designer, was sitting on the clifftop eating his sandwiches. The meeting he had been attending had adjourned for lunch and he needed some fresh air. He sat on a seat looking out to sea, and as he started to eat his lunch, the air was filled with seagulls who seemed to think it was lunchtime for them too. Still deep in thought over things that had been said at the meeting, he threw some crusts to the seagulls and was thrilled to see the speed and agility with which the birds swooped in to take the bread. They seemed to be able to just drop sideways somehow. 'WATCH THE BIRDS' the boy had said.

And so, he did. It was there and then that the idea for the Spitfire was born.

CHAPTER TEN

It took Henry quite a long time to get used to the heavy ball that was used for football in the 1940s. It was made of tough leather and inside was a rubber bladder, like a thick balloon. This was pushed into the empty leather football and it was then inflated to the correct pressure, with a bicycle pump and special adapter. When this had been achieved, the tube of the bladder was sealed off by folding it over and binding it with a fine string to stop the air escaping. It was then popped down into the football and covered with the tongue, then the slit was laced over with stitches, much the same as a shoe, except you had to use a lacer which was a large steel needle with a wooden handle to pull the laces tight. After this, all that remained to do, was to push and pommel the ball back into shape around the lace-hole until it was fairly round in shape, and there you have it, ready to play football.

The trouble was, when the ball got wet it was much heavier and really hurt if you headed it, especially if you happened to catch the lace on your forehead. But, then as now, it was the same for both sides and Henry recalled playing in a game in his former life and hearing one of the spectators, someone's Grandad no doubt, saying,

'That ball is like a Beach Ball, wasn't like that in my day.'

However, this is today and not 2012, and Coley Boys are being beaten 4-3 in the most important game Henry has played for them, the semi-final of the Berkshire Cup. They were playing Whitley Wanderers at Prospect Park and although they were a goal down, they had a slight advantage, as they were playing downhill in the second half. With five minutes to go, the heavy pitch and muddy conditions were beginning to take their toll on the Wanderers. Henry found some space on the right wing, and free of mud, he was able to run with the ball down field. The big left back came charging over, looking determined to stop him at all costs. He charges in with a sliding tackle, both feet off the ground with studs showing, A tackle that, had it connected, would've broken one or both of Henry's legs. Luckily, Henry had seen it coming. He pushed the ball up the wing and jumped high in the air, leaping completely over the charging defender. He cut inside and with only the keeper to beat, raced into the box. The keeper advanced with arms outstretched, Henry pushed the ball to his right and was about to hit it home into the net when the keeper dived for the ball and clasped it in his arms. But he'd taken Henry's legs at the same time, sending him sprawling in the mud.

'PENALTY!' Shouted everyone watching.

The ref agreed, and after a blast on his whistle, called on the trainer. He ran onto the pitch carrying a bucket of water with a sponge in it, known as 'the magic sponge.' However, after just one minute of treatment, the ref insisted Henry should leave the field and be treated on the side line. Although he was a bit shaken, Henry thought he was okay to carry on once the trainer had washed the mud away from his eyes and mouth.

'What's the score?' He asked the trainer.

'Well, it's four each now. The skipper just scored from a penalty. Are you sure you're alright?'

'Yes. I'll be fine.' Henry said. So, the trainer caught the ref's attention and he signalled the okay for Henry to go back on.

'Go to it Henry boy, we don't want it to go into extra time.' Said the trainer.

'How long have we got ref?' asked Henry, as he passed him on the way.

'Three minutes,' he said, as he blew his whistle for a free-kick inside the Wanderers half.

The entire team crowded into the box, but when the ball was pumped in, it fell to a Whitley defender who booted back up field. Everybody ran back the other way and the ball went out for a goal-kick. The manager and trainer on the touchline were going frantic,

'Keep your shape, you back four. Stay alert, read the game, and mark your man! Charging forward like that almost threw the game away.'

Just then, Henry received the ball on the halfway line and darted forward with it, as fast as his legs could carry him. Once again, the big full-back came rushing over like a charging bull. Henry slipped the ball past him and it skidded on towards the goal line. The referee looked at his watch and put the whistle to his lips and blew. Henry's shoulders dropped. 'So close,' he thought. 'But wait, he's blown for a corner!' The box was crowded now and lots of pushing and shoving was going on. Henry stood back, on the edge of the penalty area, making his run as he saw the ball come in at about shoulder height. He had almost gone in too far, but with his back to goal, he rifled the ball into the back of the net with a rolling overhead kick.

'GOAL!! We're in the final!' they all shouted.

'Do you know where the final is to be played?' said the excited manager. 'It's Elm Park. That guy from the Reading Chronicle just told me. He wants to interview one or two of you, especially you Henry.'

'Did you say Elm Park?' said one of the boys. 'THE Elm Park, home of Reading FC?'

'Yes.'

'Wow, who have we got in the final?'

'We don't know yet, but it will be either Caversham Wasps or Newbury Town.'

Henry could see the man from the Chronicle coming and he did not like the idea of answering his questions, it might be embarrassing. He turned and left the park, picked up his bag and clothes, jumped on his bike and rode swiftly home.

'Oh, my goodness look at the state of you,' said Mary. 'You'd better go round to the back door and get that kit off in the laundry room, and some of that mud as well. Before you get into the bath.'

'Yes. But Mary, Mary. We won! We are in the final. I scored the winning goal. Will you and George come to see us play?'

'In the final, yes of course we will.'

'That's good, we all get two tickets each.'

'That's fine,' said Mary. 'Now go and get yourself cleaned up, the tea's ready. We have rabbit pie tonight.'

All professional football had been suspended at the outbreak of war, because able-bodied men were required to fight for their country. However, most football stadiums stayed open and were used for charity matches and friendlies. Army teams from Aldershot and the Brock Barracks would supply teams to play at Elm Park, and sometimes the team had one or two first division players making a guest appearance. A rare treat for the local crowd. Reading, whose team in peacetime played in the third division south, had on one occasion a first division star making a guest appearance; it was a certain Matt Busby, another was Tony McFee. In addition to these friendlies, American football was played at the park. So, the pitch was marked out for both games and stayed like it all the time. The grass itself always looked immaculate, in spite of the Americans trying to dig it up with their strange brand of football. Why they even called it football is a mystery. However, a local company, Sutton Seeds, looked after the pitch and it was always the best place for miles around, and the next match scheduled to play on the lush green pitch was a Berkshire boys cup final, in ten days' time.

'Training will be on Wednesday evening; you must be there' Henry remembered the trainer saying. So, he turned up in spite of the pouring rain, he didn't have far to come, after all. But only two other boys and the trainer made it. 'Might as well go home boys, we can't do much in this weather. Just make sure you get here, whatever the weather, next Wednesday evening. It's our last chance to practice before the match. Even if we can't train, we will have a team talk.'

'Just think,' said one of Henry's teammates. 'Playing at Elm Park, on a proper pitch with terraces and a big wooden stand.'

'Yes,' said Henry. There won't be any bumps and puddles to worry about either, not like here.'

'No,' said the other boy. 'We'll have nets up on the goals too. Do you know who we are playing yet?'

'No. Not yet. We'll have to wait until Sunday to find out. But they say Caversham Wasps are much better than Newbury town and that they should get through.'

The news came through on Sunday evening; they were to play against Caversham Wasps. The following Wednesday morning, Henry woke up and was unwell with sickness and a stomach upset. On Mary's orders, he stayed in bed all day. She insisted he take some vile tasting medicine that she produced from the cupboard in the kitchen, but it worked and by 5 o'clock that evening he was feeling much better.

'Can I go to football training now?' asked Henry.

'No-no-no, you most certainly cannot.' said Mary. There was no way of getting around it, so Henry missed training. On Thursday morning he was back to normal.

'I think you get too worked up about this football thing,' said Mary at breakfast. 'You've got another two days yet before you play.' 'THING' said Henry, feeling quite indignant. 'Yes,' said Mary. 'It's only a game you know.'

Two hours before kick-off the teams gathered in the dressing rooms and Coley, having won the toss, were deemed to be the home team.

'Ere, did you see the size of some of those boys, they ain't arf big' remarked one of the Coley players 'One of them looked about 16.'

The manager clapped his hand and said,

'Never mind all that, get around the board. This is the team; Sam you get the green jersey you're in goal, left and right backs the Becket brothers' and so on. All the shirts were hanging on pegs around the room, they were red, no names, just numbers on the back, from 1 to 11. Centre forward number nine as always, eleven left wing, seven right wing, but when it came to Henry's favourite position, inside right, the shirt was given to a boy called Les Brooks.

'I'm sorry Henry you're on the bench.' He handed him a red shirt with no number on. 'You did miss training Henry.'

'Well, yes. But I did turn up the week before and hardly anybody else did.' Henry moaned.

'Yes, but we're also worried you may not be one hundred percent fit after being ill. Mervin you're on the bench too.'

Ten minutes to go and the two teams start to line up in the tunnel and it was true, they did look like a big team but 'never mind' thought Henry 'the bigger they are the harder they fall.' The ref came to the front with his two linesmen carrying a brand-new shiny ball. 'Ready boys?' he asked 'Then let's go' They marched out onto the pitch and the mighty crowd of almost 2000 burst into an air shattering roar. The game was on, the first 20 minutes was a bit of a bore, with neither side wanting to make a mistake or be too adventurous. Then Brooks, out on the right wing breezed past his man and when he was one-on-one with the keeper calmly slotted the ball home from 10 yards, ONE NIL. Coley Boys were in the lead and 15 minutes later they scored again from a corner TWO NIL.

The score stayed like that until half-time.

'Any injuries?' Asked the trainer.

'No, they all seem to be okay.'

The boys were given a mug of tea with lots of sugar, although it was scarce in wartime, but it gave the boys energy and this was an important match. Another rare treat was half an orange and there weren't many of those about during the war either. After a few words of advice here and there to individual players, the manager said,

'Right, pay attention, let's have the same again second-half. Don't lose your shape, keep your concentration.'

They went out for the second half and were greeted by a loud cheer, which was a little unfortunate for the Spring Gardens brass band, who were playing during the half-time interval, because they had not completed the last tune and had to be hurried off the pitch before the match could restart. Coley Boys were now kicking towards the Reading end, and after just two minutes of the second-half the Wasps conceded a third goal, a poor kick from the keeper gifted Coley the easiest goal of the game. The ball went to the Outside Left who drifted inside and was unmarked. He said 'thank you very much' and calmly tapped into the bottom left-hand corner. THREE NIL 'Easy Easy' shouted the crowd and so it was. But winning three nil with 40 minutes to go, the Coley players started to relax. This gave the Wasps fresh hope and they started to mount attack after attack, and five minutes later they scored with a looping header over the keeper. THREE ONE, and two minutes after that PENALTY! The cry went up as the Wasps centre forward was brought down in the area. The Coley keeper had no chance from the penalty THREE TWO and now with only four minutes left the Coley boys had to face another wave of attacks. From the bench, they could see the danger; the centre forward was completely unmarked when he received the ball BANG... THREE ALL and the whistle blew for full time. EXTRA TIME now, both teams have given their all and are in no shape to play another half hour, but rules are rules and after a short break they wearily took to the field again. Both sides came close to scoring but at the interval they were still level.

'Henry, get your boots on. Give it your best shot son.' Said the manager, as he pulled-off one of his forwards. 'We've got fifteen minutes left.'

Henry's fresh legs were no match for the opposing full-back as he sped past him time and time again. His first shot on goal was saved by the keeper, his second was way too high and he watched the spectators behind the goal all hold their heads in their hands. The next time he received the ball he decided to go through the middle, the defender facing him was already back-pedalling and Henry found it easy to send him the wrong way. As he pushed on past him, he saw him fall on his backside. Now a second defender was in his way but the boy was so tired that he could not keep up with Henry as he pushed the ball out towards the left corner flag and sped past him then, then turn towards the goal and unleash a curling shot across the keeper who stood rooted to the spot and watched in amazement as the ball curled and dipped into the far corner of the net. GOAL! This time, the fans put their hands high in the air. Coley Boys are in the lead again, with seven minutes to go.

From the kick-off, the Caversham team surged en-masse towards Coley's goal, only their keeper stayed back, and he was almost on the halfway line. With six minutes to go they're awarded a corner, the penalty box was packed, players were pushing and shoving as the ball came in, up went the heads GOAL but wait a minute…. The Ref had blown for a foul not a goal.

When the dust settled, Coley's poor goalkeeper was still lying on the ground. There were no bones broken but his back was hurt, he could not carry on. The manager put on the last sub and when he came on, he ran up to Henry and said,

'The manager wants you to go in goal.'

'Me?' said Henry.

'Yes, he said he can trust you to keep them out.'

'Gulp' went Henry, as he pulled on the keeper's jersey and gloves.

'You ready, son?' asked the ref.

'Yes, he's ready,' said the team captain. 'How long've we got?'

'Four minutes,' the ref replied.

The game restarted with a free-kick to Coley, it was taken by the new sub as he was a big strong lad and punted the ball almost to the halfway line but the ball was picked up by Caversham and back it came again. The big centre forward came charging down on Henry's goal and unleashed a stinging shot just to his right but it was a good height and he was able to get his body behind it, like all keepers are told to do. It hurt like mad but he saved the shot. Two minutes to go now and back they came again; the centre forward pushed the ball out onto the right wing and then raced in on goal to await the cross. Henry saw it coming and raced out of his area and headed the ball out for a throw-in. With plenty of players in the box, the ball was booted goalwards after the throw-in and struck a defender on the arm. PENALTY the ref pointed to the spot.

'How long, ref?' someone shouted out.

'We're in the last minute now, but you have time to take the kick.'

'Oh blast, so near and yet so far. If they score now, we go to penalties.' Said one of the boys.

'Come ON Henry, you can save this!'

The ball was on the spot, the ref ushering the players back behind the ball, Henry stood on his line. 'I know which way I'm going' he said to himself as the ref blew. The striker made his run and the ball flew low, towards the corner. It was one foot above the ground, to Henry's right, which was the way he'd decided to dive. His right hand just got the ball but he couldn't stop it. In a heart stopping moment he watched as the ball deflected onto the post and rebounded into his arms. The shot was saved!! Three long blasts on the ref's whistle signified the end of the match; Coley had won the cup. Henry was soon buried under a pile of grateful teammates.

'Let me up!' He shouted. 'I can hardly breathe down here.'

Eventually, the celebrating eased and Henry was able to get to his feet again. The manager and trainer were both on the pitch, overjoyed at the team's performance and of course the win.

'Well done lads,' said the manager. 'As for hero-Henry, what can I say after a performance like that. You will go down as super-sub from now on. Come on now, we have to get lined up for the presentation of the cup.' Getting the two teams to line up for the presentation was quite a task as Coley were still on a high but Caversham would've preferred to just go home. But at long last they managed to get them in one single line facing the small deputation from the town hall. The guest of honour was the mayor, who shook hands with both teams and presented Coley Boys with the cup. Not exactly the FA Cup you understand but by the way those boys celebrated that afternoon it could well have been.

CHAPTER ELEVEN

The year was now 1941 and Henry was still being schooled at home. Mary was an excellent teacher and was still very strict regarding school hours and even homework. Although he was the only pupil in the class, he still had to raise his hand to ask a question, which seemed a bit silly. Mary, or 'Miss' as she was addressed in school, insisted on it.

'We don't want you growing up with bad manners, whatever would they say when you get back ho....'

She tried to stop herself saying it but it just come out. She had still not come to terms with the fact the boy could've come from the future and so she had programmed her mind to think of him as just another evacuee.

'You still don't believe me, do you?' Henry said.

'Well, it's not that I don't want to believe, because I do want to, but it is inconceivable that I....'

Henry broke in and said,

'I think I can prove it to you if I can get my mobile charged, but I haven't got a charger.'

'Why don't we ask George if one of his people at work can help?'

When they asked George that evening, he said,

'Well, perhaps one of John's boffins could find a way, but all that modern stuff you possess is quite bewildering, show me the battery. What a tiny little thing. Is it 230 volts?'

'I suppose so.' Henry replied, and then added,

'No, wait. It might be 12 volt, my aunt used to charge her phone in the car.'

'How on earth did she do that?' Asked George.

'She just plugged it into the cigarette lighter.'

George and Mary just looked at each other and shook their heads.

'I will get John to have a look at it for you, and see if he can charge it up. But I don't see how you're going to phone someone with it if you can't phone them with that.' He said, pointing to the phone on the sideboard. With that, he put the battery in his pocket and said, 'Leave it with me.'

When George returned home that evening, Mary greeted him with,

'Any luck dear?'

'With what?' He asked.

'The battery of course.'

'Oh, no. Not yet I'm afraid. John said he might be able to do something though. He's working on it but don't get your hopes up too high, Mary. Even if this phone works, he can't phone somebody 70 years hence, can he?'

Two days later, George returned from his place of work with a fully charged battery.

'Hello Mary,' he said. 'Where is Henry?

'He's in his room, doing his homework.'

'Ask him to come down, will you please? And tell him to bring his phone. I'll pour us both a drink in the lounge.'

Henry appeared in the lounge before George had poured the drinks.

'Did you get it charged?' He asked, excitedly.

'All in good time.' George said. 'Take a seat and wait for Mary.'

Mary came in one minute later.

'Here's your drink dear.' He said, handing her a sherry.

'What about Henry?' Mary asked.

'No. He doesn't want anything at the moment, do you lad?'

'No thank you, but can we please try the battery?'

'Okay,' said George. Producing it from his pocket, he held it up in front of Henry's face and said 'Henry, you've told us that by using this phone you can somehow prove all that you have been telling us about yourself and your past history. Both Mary and I have been hoping against hope that you can do so. We want so much for you to be right, for your sake as well as ours. Here is your battery Henry, make your call.'

Henry took the battery and slipped it into the phone, replaced the back and pressed the on/off switch. The phone started up with a ping-pong sound. The two adults looked at each other, wondering what else they were going to hear.

'I think it would be better if I sat on the settee, between you both.' Henry said. 'Well, here goes.'

He slid the phone open, pressed the menu button, selected camera and then 'my pictures.'

'Okay,' he said. 'Can you see that alright? It's a picture of me on my bike, outside my house and you can see the number there. Look on the wall, it's twenty three, and here look.' He pointed to the bottom of the screen. 'The road name is Nutmeg Close.'

Silence, then George said,

'Well, I do declare. That is amazing.'

'What wonderful colours.' Mary added.

'Let me see if I can find some more.' Said Henry, and found a picture of four of his school mates in the playground, all wearing the same school uniform that Henry had worn when they first met.

'This is my aunt, standing with her new Mini in Tesco's car park.'

There were lots more but George said,

'That's very convincing my boy, but how do we know they are not a bunch of fake pictures put in that little machine of yours?'

'What about this one then? I hope this will convince you.'

They were looking at a picture of Her Majesty, Queen Elizabeth II, attending the pageant on the Thames for her Diamond Jubilee. They sat there in silence, not knowing what to say. The fact that the banners on the waterfront showed the date clearly as 2012, they were still unable to take it all in.

'Right, now one more thing to convince you.' Said Henry, holding the camera arm's-length towards him and he said 'smile' and took a picture. Showing them the result, all three of them sitting together on the settee.

'Well, I'll be darned.' Said George.

Mary put both arms around Henry and gave him a big kiss, saying,

'Oh you poor boy.'

Henry broke down and cried.

'Now you believe me, don't you?'

'Yes, of course we do.' They both said at the same time.

Henry felt very relieved that they both now believed what he had been telling them.

'I'm so pleased that I was able to show you some proof, I was getting worried that I had dreamt it all. I still do not know how this has all happened to me and I'm wondering what my aunt will do when I don't arrive back from school.'

'Oh dear said Mary, I can see why you must be worried but I just don't know what we can do about it.'

'We will look after you Henry,' said George. 'I'll get some advice from my head of department and see what he can come up with. But I must say that your knowledge of this war will undoubtedly be extremely useful and a great help to the country.'

Henry felt happier than he had for days and thanked them both for their kindness to him.

'I really was very lucky when you found me, George. I will do whatever you think is best.'

'I think it's about time we went to bed, after all this excitement. We'll see what tomorrow brings.'

Henry went up to his bedroom knowing that he would be able to sleep a lot better tonight.

The following afternoon at school, Mary caught Henry looking at his mobile phone when he should've been doing his sums.

'What are you doing now Henry?'

'I'm looking to see if the calculator on here still works. This 12 times table is doing my head in. You do know this will all be redundant when we go decimal, don't you?'

'Henry my boy, you speak in riddles sometimes. I don't know what the calculator is but I want you to take that phone up to your room then come back and concentrate on your studies.'

Henry was on his way upstairs when the front door opened. George was home from work a little earlier than usual, Henry thought.

'Come in to my study.' Said George, as he closed the front door. Henry noticed a very stern look on his face and wondered what he had done wrong. As the two of them were entering the study Mary came into the hall.

'Is anything wrong dear?' She said. 'You haven't even said good evening yet.'

'I'm sorry Mary, no nothing wrong. I would like a word with young Henry though. Just give us a minute in private will you please.'

Mary looked stunned, she had often been asked to stay out of the way before when George had meetings with high ranking ministers and dignitaries but never for a school boy and her only pupil at that. It must be something serious she thought, and indeed it was.

'Come in and sit down please, George said.

When they were both seated face-to-face across the desk, George continued.

'Henry, the Prime Minister wants to see you.'

'Winston Churchill?' Said a very excited Henry. 'At number 10 Downing Street?'

'The Prime Minister, yes. But not in London. The meeting will take place here, in Reading. Well not here but at the Grange. A staff car will pick us both up at 9 AM sharp.'

'Are you going to come with me then?' asked Henry.

'Oh yes, of course I am. Don't worry, it will be alright.' Replied George.

'But what does he want with me?' asked a very surprised Henry.

'Well Henry, I told him today about your phone and the pictures of your queen at the diamond jubilee pageant. He wants to see you take a picture of him and yourself together before he can take it all in. But what he wants to know most is, what does he have to do to get the USA to join this war?'

'He doesn't have to do anything.'

'No?'

'No,' continued Henry. 'The Japs are going to do that for him.'

'The Japs?'

'Yes, the Japanese.' Said Henry, then told George all about what happened at Pearl Harbour.

'When does this happen?' Demanded George.

'Sorry, I can't remember the date. But I think it's before Christmas this year.'

'Good gracious, it's December already. My word, will Winnie be pleased when he hears this! Off you go now, all Mary's homework for tonight is cancelled.

You, my boy, must concentrate all you can on this war and be ready for the meeting tomorrow. With as much as you can remember about it all.'

CHAPTER TWELVE

As expected, the car arrived on time. The driver bid the two of them good morning and held the door whilst George and Henry climbed into the back seat. The car was a large dark green Rolls Royce.

'Nice Car' George remarked to the driver.

'Yes sir, it's quite new and reserved for VIPs.'

'VIPs eh,? Well, what do you think of that, Henry my boy?'

Henry didn't seem to think too much of it at all, he'd been in deep thought.

'You will come in with me, won't you? I mean I won't have to face him on my own, will I?'

'No of course not, don't worry. I'll be with you all the time.'

They sat in silence for the rest of the journey, which was not long at all. Soon, the car pulled up in front of a pair of large iron gates which were opened by two red caps (army policeman.) Once inside, the car stopped at a checkpoint at the beginning of a long tree-lined drive. In the distance, Henry could see the grand manor house. It was built in a sand-coloured stone with its tall towers and chimneys looking magnificent in the winter sun. One of the two red-caps that had let them in took the drivers pass, studied it for a moment, and ordered the driver to wind down the blacked out rear windows of the car.

'Good morning.' He said to the two VIPs sitting in the back seat. Followed by, 'Carry on please.'

After putting the windows back to the closed position, the car moved on towards the house and the gates were closed behind them.

The main entrance to the house was very impressive; it had two huge solid oak doors that must've been hundreds of years old. These were closed but there was a small one that was open, it was set into the right-hand main door. George said,

'Do you know what that is called, Henry? That kind of door within the door'

'Is it a 'Judas Gate'?' said Henry.

'Yes, that's right.' George replied.

As they stepped into the main hall, they were approached by a tall middle-aged man. smartly dressed in a blue pinstripe suit and a dark tie, with very shiny shoes.

'Good morning George,' he said. 'This must be Henry, I suppose.' He added, in an intrigued tone. 'I am the PM's secretary, and he would like you to wait here for just a few minutes. He promised to be as quick as possible, but please take a seat.' He indicated some seats to one side of the main marble staircase. Henry could see that the landing at the top gave access to four or five other rooms, it was all very similar to a large country house his aunt had taken him to see somewhere in Berkshire, he thought. In fact, he had seen quite a few old houses in his time, because his aunt was a member of the National Trust and Henry liked to go along because he was very much into History. But the entrance hall to this house was different, there were no paintings or statues or anything of value in-sight. Apart from the ceilings, which had paintings of goddesses and hunting scenes painted by an Italian artist, he thought, but not knowing who.

'Why do you think he stared at me like that?' Henry asked George. His mind snapping-back quite suddenly to the purpose of his visit.

'I imagine he believes you've come from outer space or something?'

'The PM will see you now,' said the man in the pinstripe suit, who was at the top of the stairs now. 'Won't you come up?'

Upstairs, he ushered them into a room on the right-hand side of the landing. Winston Churchill sat behind a large desk, smoking a cigar, which had filled the room with blue smoke.

'Come on,' he called. 'Don't be afraid.' As he noticed George almost had to push Henry into the room. 'Perhaps I should be afraid of you, young man. Please sit down.' He said, motioning to the two chairs opposite him. 'We have iced water here but if you would like something else to drink I... '

'No, no.' They both shook their heads.

'Very well then, would you please leave us now, Brian?' He said to the secretary. 'I do not want to be disturbed under any circumstances, understood?'

'Very well, sir.' Said Brian, as he left the room.

When the door closed, Churchill spoke.

'So, we meet at last. My good friend George has told me an awful lot about you, Henry. But what he has been telling me, has left me lost for words. Did you bring your little camera phone with you?'

'Yes, sir.' Said Henry, hoping against hope it would still work.

'Alright, we will get to that in a moment, but what I want to know is how did you know what I was going to say in my speech to the nation, when I had not yet written it or even decided what to say?'

'Well, it's documented in history,' said Henry. 'It's a very famous speech.'

'Is it indeed?' said the Prime Minister. 'What else have you learnt in your documented history lessons?' Henry at this time was looking around the room, which prompted George to ask,

'Are you paying attention to what the Prime Minister is saying to you, Henry?'

'Yes, sorry.' Said Henry. 'But if I tell you a secret that was not made public until after the war was over, will you believe what I am saying is true?'

Churchill looked at Henry.

'I don't know what he's going to say next,' said George. 'What are you talking about, son?

'All these bare patches on the wall here, and he indicated with a sweep of his arm. You have hidden all the valuable artwork and treasure in case Hitler gets them, am I right?'

'Well, yes you are. But any fool would be able to guess that, it goes without saying that we are going to hide our national treasures in times of hostilities. So, what's your point?'

'My point, sir. Is that I know where you have hidden them.'

There was silence for a few seconds then at last the Prime Minister spoke, with uncharacteristic hesitancy.

'Even I don't know that, only a handful of people in the nation know the secret location, and I am not one of them. In case I get captured and put to torture by the Gestapo. So, tell me, how can you know?'

'We learnt about it, in World War II history, and the location is…..'

'No-no-no! Do not tell me, or anyone else for that matter. Your life would be in grave danger.'

Churchill was beginning to feel a little uncomfortable; this young whippersnapper in front of him seemed to know more about the war than he did. There was silence for a while then the PM said,

'Right. Tell me from the beginning, how did you get here?'

Henry thought for a bit and then said,

'The Rag and Bone man let me ride on his cart and….'

'No-no-no. That's not what I mean. How did you get to be here, in Reading?'

'It was 1939 when I first found him,' said George.

'Yes, that's what I want to know' said the PM. How did you come to be here, now? When you claim to be from another time?'

'I just don't know, I wish I did, then maybe I could go home again. All I know is I was born in Reading in the year 2001 and the last thing I can remember is a storm in 2012.'

'Is that what you want? To go back to the time you came from?' The Prime Minister enquired.

'I don't know. I sometimes think I was sent here to help you win this war.'

Henry looked as if he were about to cry.

After a short pause, George suggested,

'Why don't you show the PM the pictures in your phone, Henry?'

After explaining why he could not make a phone call from his phone, because the satellites had not been launched into space yet, Churchill said,

'Okay, let's move onto these pictures.' When he saw the pictures of her Majesty the Queen, he added, 'That must be the King's eldest daughter, Princess Elizabeth. It seems as if she has been on the throne for 60 years. Well I do declare.'

When Henry took a picture of all three of them together, the PM said,

'You have convinced me, Henry. Although I can't quite believe I am saying this, I am in no doubt that you have somehow come here from the future. Perhaps we will never know how you ended up here, but while you are here, you must tell us all that you can remember from your history lessons. In particular, what more do I have to do to get the Americans into this damned war?'

'You don't have to do anything, sir.' George told him. The Japs are going to sink the American Pacific Fleet, at anchor in Pearl Harbor.

'When?' asked Churchill, addressing Henry.

'Well, I don't know for sure, but it was sometime just before Christmas.'

'Let me see' said Churchill. 'It's the 8th of December today....'

Just at that moment, there was a BANG-BANG-BANG on the door, and without waiting for an answer the Prime Minister's Secretary burst into the room carrying a piece of paper.

'I thought I told you..'

'I know, sir. My apologies, but you will want to see this signal that has just come in.' The Prime Minister read aloud,

'YESTERDAY AT SEVEN A.M. DEC THE SEVENTH THE USA PACIFIC FLEET WAS SUNK AT ANCHOR BY THE JAPANESE AIR FORCE. AMERICA IS NOW AT WAR'

'Are there many casualties?' asked the PM.

'Yes, quite a lot sir, answered the Secretary. But fortunately most of the sailors were still ashore on weekend leave, or the death toll would've been considerably higher.

'Yes, I see,' said Churchill. 'However, today is beginning to be the best day of my life. I'm convinced we shall win this war now.' He made a fist and punched the air with delight, shouting YES!'

'Sir,' said Henry. 'What you must do now is ask the Russians to come in on our side too. The Prime Minister's Secretary stood with his mouth wide open. Churchill looked at him for a second or two and then said,

'Well, do it man. Get me Stalin on the phone. This boy knows what he's talking about. George, I want you to see to it that this young man signs the official secrets act and he is to be enrolled as a full member of your staff.' Turning to Henry, he said, 'Two hours ago I was the number one most wanted man in Nazi Germany, I think you've just pushed me down to number two. Now, I need to make this phone call to Moscow. While I do, I want you to make sure you've told George everything you can think of, about your phone. It may help us to solve a big problem we are having out at Bletchley Park.'

'Yes sir.' Said Henry, and after the PM had gone in to another room, he said to George 'Is he talking about the ENIGMA code?'

George pointed to a sign on the wall that said WALLS HAVE EARS and then to another that read CARELESS TALK COSTS LIVES. 'What was George worrying about?' thought Henry. It was only the three of them and the PMs secretary, that had been involved in the discussion.

All of a sudden, the red telephone on the PM's desk began to flash and George went next door, to alert him. The Prime Minister hurried back into the room and snatched up the hand set,

'Speak to me.'

Someone on the end of the line jabbered away excitedly for a few seconds, and then the PM put the phone down, saying,

'I have to return to London immediately.'

He rang for his secretary, who seemed to enter the room before the PMs fingers had left the buzzer.

'Have my car brought around, straight away. Oh, and arrange another for yourself and get straight back to London.' Snatching up his brief case, he turned to George and said 'You come with me, and bring young Henry. We shall continue hearing this amazing story of yours on the way.' Inside of the Rolls Royce that smelled strongly of old leather and cigar smoke, Henry was sitting across from George and the PM. The driver was on his own in the front, behind a sound proof screen. As they left Reading and sped along the A4, towards Maidenhead, the PM said,

'Tell me, Henry. What else can you do with this magic gadget of yours?'

'It's not magic sir. It's just a phone.'

'Just a phone, eh? I understand you can't show me how it works, is that right?'

'I'm afraid not sir. As I said, It relies on technology that just doesn't exist yet, especially the satellites required to carry the signal.'

'Of course,' said the PM. 'Now, am I to understand that in the land where you come from, everyone has one of these?'

'Yes, sir. But I don't come from another land. I come from here, in Reading.' Tears started to fill his eyes.

'OK-OK' the PM said. 'I'm sorry Henry, this is still taking some getting used to. Lets get back to what this phone of yours can do.'

'Yes, sir. They're actually called smartphones, because of all the things you can do with them. But most people still refer to them as phones, or mobiles. Other than making calls, which people do less and less in 2012, you are able to send each other emails and text messages, from phone to phone. They are a bit like telegrams, but they arrive instantly, in the palm of your hand, no matter where you are in the world, and they can be thousands of words long. People often include photographs and videos with the messages too. But that's nothing, I used to make video phone calls to my friends, so they could see me as well as hear me, like a movie! People also use their phones to find their way around, either when they're driving or walking. There are moving maps on your phone that come with spoken and written directions, like having your own navigator. The map always knows where you are, which is so clever. It's all to do with something called GPS, it uses the satellites I mentioned before, which are machines up in space, orbiting the Earth like the Moon, sending signals down to your phone. It's so useful for my schoolwork too, first of all, my teacher sets the homework so everybody in the class can see it on their phone. That way they don't have to remember it or rush to write it down at the end of the lesson. Their parents can check it from their phones too, so they know what work their children should be doing. But not only that, there's a thing called Google. Apparently, it's named after an enormous number, because of all the information it can help you find. It's like the world's biggest encyclopaedia, but you access it all from your phone. There are so many other things too, you can order your dinner to be delivered to your door, share all of your photos for your friends and family to see. My Aunt's friend Reg, even uses his to find sheet music and tune his guitar.'

The car had now reached the outskirts of London, around Hammersmith, and Henry was shocked at the ruins and shells of people's homes that littered both sides of the road. There was nothing left apart from the occasional chimney stack, or maybe the remains of a staircase. In some places, the fires from incendiary bombs were still smouldering. It was truly devastating, not only on the outskirts but all the way into the city. Henry could see that both George and Churchill were deeply moved.

'They're going to pay for this,' said Churchill, 'you wait and see.'

All of a sudden, the wailing of the Air Raid siren screeched out, another bombing raid was about to happen.

'To the War Rooms, quick as you can driver, they are just around the corner.' Urged the PM. 'As he spoke, the Roller screeched to a halt outside the entrance to the War Rooms. 'Quick, George. Bring your nephew with you,' said the Prime Minister. The nephew bit was for the benefit of the driver who was holding open the car door.

Once inside, they descended deep underground. The Cabinet and War Rooms, as they were known, were a labyrinth of rooms and corridors that stretched under Westminster. There were many people buzzing about and after a bit, Churchill found a young lady in a Wren uniform, and said to Henry,

'This young lady is going to find you a nice quiet spot to wait.' Turning to the Wren, he said, 'Find him something to read and perhaps a cup of tea if he wants one.'

'Yes, of course. Would you like one sir?'

'You're joking, aren't you? Come on George we'll find some scotch and don't worry about the bombs Henry. You are quite safe down here...'

As he spoke, there was the most horrendous explosion and everything seemed to shake.

'Wow! What on earth are they dropping on us now?' shouted George.

'I think it must have been a landmine.' Henry observed.

Churchill was just about to ask 'What on earth..?' but George caught him by the arm and said,

'Do you see what I mean? Come on, where is that scotch?'

Henry thought to himself, 'this place is not the same as it looked on my school trip.' He was referring to the noise and pandemonium, the alarm bells, the typewriters and ticker tape machines, messengers running about with signals and top secret bits of paper. It was hot and humid, and a smell came from a broken sewer pipe somewhere. He didn't like it at all. Not only that, bits of white dust and plaster from the ceiling had dropped into his tea.

The bombing had stopped and things had quietened down a little when George reappeared.

'We can go back home as soon as the all-clear sounds, Henry. It won't be long now.'

'It can't come soon enough for me,' Henry thought. As they spoke, the wail of the all-clear siren drifted across the city and the bombproof doors to the shelter were opened. The driver came to join them, and all three walked out, and up to the street, into a scene of utter chaos. They picked their way through fallen masonry and rubble, to look for the car. They found it upside down at the bottom of a bomb crater that was about half the size of an Olympic swimming pool. Others joined them to look down into the hole and Henry became aware that the man standing next to him was hanging on to his arm, before he gradually began to slip to the ground.

'He's fainted.' Shouted Henry, as George knelt down and loosened the man's tie.

'Get some water, somebody. Quick.'

Then a voice commanded,

'Stand back, I'm a doctor'

It had come from a man with a black bag in his hand. Kneeling down beside the stricken man, he took out a stethoscope and duly checked the man's heartrate and breathing (who by this time had begun to look a pallid shade of grey.) It wasn't long before the doctor took the stethoscope from his ears, popped it back into the black bag, and announced that the man had died from a heart attack. With that, he promptly walked back into the shelter.

The news brought an 'oh' and mutters of 'what a shame' and the like, but most people drifted away, apart from a few that seemed to know him. Judging by how visibly upset they were.

'Come on,' said George. 'Nothing we can do here.'

'No wait, please.' Henry said 'Let me try the kiss of life.'

'Whatever did the boy mean? George thought. But he let him get on with it.

Kneeling beside the corpse, Henry pinched the man's nose with his left forefinger and thumb, held open his mouth with the other hand and then proceeded to blow deep breaths into the man's lungs. At that moment, one of the people watching tried to gently lift Henry away saying,

'Come on son, the man's dead' but George intervened.

'No, please let the boy try'.

Henry had stopped blowing into the man's lungs now and was sitting astride the body. With both hands, one on top of the other, he was giving rhythmic hard pushes on the man's chest. After about ten pushes, he stopped and then put his ear to the chest and listened, nothing. He went back to pushing the chest again, then had another listen. This time he heard a faint heartbeat and a broad smile began to spread across the boy's face. He stood up as the man started to show signs of life, there were gasps from the crowd when the so-called dead-man started to stir, like a modern-day Lazarus.

'But the Doctor said he was dead!' Cried out one man.

'Who is this boy?' asked another.

George grabbed Henry by the collar and dragged him through the crowd. The pair quickly crossed the road and disappeared into the park.

Just where did you learn to do that?' George asked.

'St Johns Ambulance,' came the reply. 'Hey was that good or what!'

CHAPTER THIRTEEN

The following day, Henry was taken by George back to The Grange, the large house where he'd been introduced to Winston Churchill. It was hard to believe that was only yesterday; so much had happened in the meantime.

After the morning meeting with the Prime Minister, Henry left the office with George. As they walked down the great staircase, George said,

'Now I know you have a great deal to think about, and it must be said that you are probably the youngest person in history to be asked to sign the official secrets act, but try not to let it worry you. Just concentrate on your World War II history lessons, and tell us anything and everything that you can remember. But you may only talk about it with the Prime Minister, and myself. That's really important, Henry.'

'How come you know him?' Henry asked.

'Oh, we were at school together, at Harrow.'

They reached the bottom of the stairs and George pointed to a poster on the wall, it read

CARELESS TALK COSTS LIVES

'I want you to remember that,' said George. 'Don't even tell Mary about anything that goes on in this house, and certainly don't speak about it to your friend Kate.'

'But she lives here.' said Henry.

'Well, yes I know. But Lady Palmer, who is the owner of the house, lives only in the west wing. She lives there with Kate and three servants. The rest of the house she has donated to the government. You can't get to the west wing from here, you have to go out of the grounds and all the way round the estate and enter by the west gate. The grounds too have been separated by that high wall there, so you can't tell from outside that it has two separate entries. Right, what I am going to show you now may come as a bit of a shock. But we feel, as you are to be part of the school, you should be entitled to know what goes on here. Come with me.'

Henry followed George out of the front door, into the vast grounds of the house. About 30 yards away from the door was a large cluster of rhododendron bushes and almost hidden in them was a garden shed. It was locked and George produced a key from his pocket, unlocked the door and went inside.

'Come on in,' he said to Henry, who wondered what he was going to see inside the shed. 'Shut the door please, Henry.'

George instructed. With the door closed, the inside of the shed was quite dark, but from somewhere George produced a small torch and Henry could now see a rather dirty old mat on the floor. What he couldn't see was the trap door beneath it, which opened when George removed the mat, to reveal a narrow flight of stairs, leading down. At the bottom was the entrance to a tunnel that was not quite high enough for George to stand up in, so he led the way with knees bent and head bowed. Henry didn't have to stoop but he did anyway.

At the end of the tunnel was a steel door, with a combination-coded lock. George punched in some numbers and the heavy steel door swung open. The two of them stepped inside a small room with a couple of shelves, a small storage cupboard, and a door marked W.C. At the end of the room was another steel door but no keyhole or combination-lock. George gave four sharp taps and waited until he heard three taps in reply. Seemingly, this was the 'okay to enter' signal and George slowly pushed the heavy door open.

'At ease men,' said George to the three men in the room. Once inside, the door was closed behind them with a reassuring thud.

The young man who had let them in joined the others at the table in the centre of the room and resumed his studies. All three men looked very young; in fact the one who had opened the door for them looked hardly any older than Henry. George walked round the room, pointing things out as he went,

'Kitchen in there, here's the toilet, there's the wash-basin, and store cupboard etc etc. Come this way' he said, as he opened the door at the far end of the room.

Before going through it he took out his torch and switched it on. Henry could see they were in a rough narrow tunnel and it seemed as if it was sloping downhill. As they slowly inched along, stooped almost double, Henry wondered where on earth they were headed, and how long it had taken to dig this tunnel. After a little way, the tunnel felt as if it was levelling-out and in two or three minutes, the path they were treading seemed to be rising. 'We are going up now; thank goodness,' thought Henry, as he bumped into George who had stopped to unbolt the door. With a shove, George opened the door, letting them out into the fresh air.

'One of my instructors will secure the door to the escape shortly. Now, as you can see, we are on the opposite side of the house from where we went in. Please dust yourself off, as we are going back into the house using this side entrance,' explained George.

Along a short passage they came to a door that had a notice on it, that read,

KNOCK BEFORE ENTERING

George knocked, but as he got no answer, he went in and held the door open for Henry. The room was large with a centre table and 10 chairs.

'Sit down Henry, would you like a drink?'

'Yes. Some water, please.' Henry had become quite thirsty when he saw the jug of iced water on the table. As they sat down, George poured the water.

'Got any questions?'

'Have I got..?' and Henry stopped short when he saw the grin on George's face.

The grin faded and George became deadly serious,

'Henry,' he said. 'This is a bad war we are in, and it's a dirty war. The dirty part of it, is what we do here. Those underground rooms you have just seen, are the rooms where we train all our agents, spies and saboteurs. By the time they leave here, they are fully trained in unarmed combat explosives, coded messaging and decoding. They will know how to kill a sentry without a sound, where to place explosive charges for the best effect, and many other invaluable things. All these men are volunteers and are too young to be in the army but joined the home guard and were vetted and chosen from there. One more thing, if a soldier is captured on enemy soil, he's taken prisoner. But if a spy is captured, he or she is shot. Now 'what's all this got to do with me' you are thinking, right? Well, don't worry. We aren't going to make you a spy. Do you remember the young man who opened the door for us down below?'

'Yes,' said Henry.

'Well, he is being trained for a very high priority mission in France. However, his French is good but it is not of-the-region.'

'What region is it,' asked Henry?

'Well, it's where your aunt comes from, and you have the dialect. What's more, you've been there before, haven't you?'

'How has he remembered all that?' thought Henry, but asked, 'Do you want me to go with him?'

'No Henry, we couldn't risk that. We just want you to help us train him. Help him to perfect the necessary dialect and tell him all you can about the area. Can you do that?'

'What's the man's name?' Henry asked.

George looked at him and said,

'He is 864 and you are 865'

'Wow,' thought Henry. A long way from 007.

CHAPTER FOURTEEN

Kate's bedroom is directly above Lady Palmer's lounge in the West Wing of the great house. It overlooks the lawns and driveway that leads to the very impressive front entrance. The lounge itself was a very elegant room, tastefully furnished, and it housed a beautiful white grand piano. A present, Kate was given to understand, from an American musician by the name of Jerome Kern. Kate sometimes lay in bed at night listening to Lady Palmer playing, the sounds seemed to rise-up the chimney and flood into Kate's bedroom from the fireplace. The music was not the only sound that rose-up the chimney. When Lady Palmer was entertaining, Kate could often hear the voices of her guests, who tended to be VIPs, including film stars, politicians, and sometimes even royalty. Kate was not a nosy girl by nature but sometimes when she knew there were very famous people downstairs, she could not resist sitting close to the fireplace.

One Saturday morning late in December, Kate saw George, the man she had come to know as Henry's guardian, approaching the front of the house. This wasn't unusual in itself, Kate had seen him at the west wing a few times before, but she thought he had a worried look on his face, as he walked up the driveway. After a short space of time (enough time Kate thought for him to get into the lounge below) she placed herself on her chair by the fireplace. Unfortunately, the sound was not very good on that particular day, though. She could hear the two voices but could not make out what they were saying. Then she heard Lady Palmer,

'YOU'VE DONE WHAT? What on earth do you mean? Have you gone raving mad?' George said something but Kate couldn't hear, but she did hear Lady Palmer reply with, 'I don't care what the Prime Minister says, I am Head of this school and I cannot sanction this. Furthermore..' Kate did not hear the rest of the conversation, but she did catch the last bit. Lady Palmer's voice was raised again, 'and I want him here ready to move in by Monday morning do I make myself clear?'

'I wonder what that was all about,' thought Kate as she sat down on her bed. 'I've never heard Lady Palmer raise her voice before, she is normally so quiet and lady-like. Whatever it was that George had done, must have been serious to cause her to react like that.' Another thing Kate couldn't understand was that George had always seemed such a perfect gentleman, so what could he have done and who were they talking about? Who could be moving in on Monday? Surely not Henry, George's evacuee? 'That would be nice,' she thought, but Henry had always said how happy he was living with Mary and George at Coley. 'Oh well, I will just have too wait and see, one more mystery in this strange house.' Kate thought. She knew she was looking forward to the outcome though, especially if it turned out to be her friend Henry who was to move in.

Henry moved into The Grange (west wing) as instructed, first thing Monday morning. Along with Shep and his bicycle, he brought all of his worldly goods and belongings (his clothes and football kit) packed in a small suitcase, together with his schoolbooks from past and present.

'The dog can't stay,' were Lady Palmer's first words. Henry's face dropped.

'No-no, I'm afraid not. I don't want that dog worrying my deer herd, or my horses. I am sorry Henry, but the dog must go back.' Henry took a deep breath and said,

'Then I cannot stay either.' What Henry did not know of course was that Lady Palmer had spent two hours on the phone the previous evening to the Prime Minister, with the intention of giving him a piece of her mind, and pointing out that as head of M.I.5. she did not take kindly to being treated in this way. The very idea that this young boy should become a member of the department without consulting her, was unprecedented.

'Madam, Madam,' the P.M. had said, as soon as there was a break in the verbal chastising he was receiving. 'First of all, as your Prime Minister, I order you to calm down. Goodness knows I have enough worries and trouble coming from the Germans, I can't have trouble from within too. Now, let me tell you just what we have decided to do with young Henry. Because of his specialised knowledge of this war and of Northern France, along with his excellent command of the language, he has been engaged as my personal advisor and in an advisory position for two of your Special Agents undergoing training at the moment. You will no doubt know which two I mean. One more thing, George has arranged a meeting with you for tomorrow lunchtime, yes? Then at that meeting you will find out just why this young man is so important to us and I am all in favour of the boy living with you at The Grange, all the better for us to look after him. By the way, he will bring his dog.'

The PM put the receiver back on its cradle before she could protest.

When Henry told her he couldn't stay without the dog, she recalled the P.M.'s words the night before 'he will bring his dog.'

'How do you know he will not chase my deer?' asked Lady Palmer.

'Because I will tell him not to.'

'Oh, you will, will you?'

'Yes. I promise you he will not worry your sheep, horses, or deer. Please let him stay,' pleaded Henry.

'Well, alright. Let's give it a trial. I will give him two weeks, what do you think of that?' Asked Lady Palmer.

'Oh, thank you miss!' said Henry.

'It's ma'am, not miss. You must call me ma'am, I'm your boss now.' she interrupted.

'Yes ma'am' Henry answered, just like on New Tricks or The Bill, because they always call their bosses ma'am when they are women, he thought to himself. Henry had been to the west wing quite a few times now and he had been invited into the large reception hall whilst waiting for Kate but never any more than that, he had not seen much of the rest of the house or grounds, although he did know about the horses because Kate had told him she was learning to ride.

'Now let me show you to your room,' said Lady Palmer. 'This way, bring your things.' She led the way in to the house and up the grand staircase to the first floor 'This will be your room,' she announced. Stopping at the first door on the right.

'And that's Kates room there,' she noted. Indicating the door opposite.

When Henry first looked into his room, he was pleasantly surprised

'Wow. That's cool,' he said when he saw the four-poster bed.

'Oh, do you think its cold in there? I thought it was quite warm, you have the morning sun on the side of the house.'

'No, no. I didn't mean that it was cold. Cool means that something is good.'

'Does it really? Your bathroom is in here.' Adding under her breath as she opened the door to the en-suite, 'They told me he says some strange things now and again.' The bathroom was in fact almost as big as the bedroom and had a sunken bath. It wasn't like some of the bathrooms he'd seen in old country houses, this was wonderful with blue and white tiles and the bath itself was white marble and had gold taps that looked like fishes. 'Do you think this is also cool?' She asked when she saw the look on the boy's face.

'It's wicked' came the reply.

'That's funny, I thought he liked it,' thought Lady Palmer.

'We have a meeting with George at lunchtime, but that leaves us a couple of hours yet. Would you like me to get my bike out? We could have a look at the grounds together. Then Kate can show you the rest of the house when she comes home from school?'

'Yes, that will be nice.' Said Henry.

'Let's go then. We can do the Deer Park first, and then if we ride all the way round the lake, we can do the stables on the way home.'

'I didn't know you had a lake here,' said Henry.

'Oh yes, it's deep in the woods and very beautiful. It's full of fish too, trout mostly, do you like trout?'

'I don't know,' answered Henry. I don't think I have ever tasted it.

'Goodness me, never had trout before, eh? Well, I will ask Cook to put them on the menu next week if you like. But of course, it will mean that you and I must catch some. What do you think of that, Henry?'

'Sounds cool, I've never caught a fish before.' He replied.

The deer, when they got close, were very nervous. But they didn't move too far, which surprised Lady P as they usually bounded away when approached, and would never come too close to the wire fence. Henry and Lady P stood and watched some groups of three or four in the background, leaping about and chasing from one spot to another.

'Do you like venison Henry?' Lady P asked, and without waiting for an answer said, 'You probably will before you leave here.'

Just then Henry noticed a man walking towards them, he had a shot gun cradled over his right arm.

'Morning ma'am,' he called as he approached.

'Good morning, Oliver. This is Henry' she said. 'Henry. This is Oliver, my gamekeeper.'

'How do you do young man, are you the new evacuee Cook was telling me about?' And to Lady P he said 'We lost another young fawn last night ma'am.'

'Same thing again?' she asked.

'Yep. Same thing again. It's either a wolf or a big cat by the looks of things. Maybe more than one. I heard they lost a couple of young sheep last week, over at Bucknell's farm.'

'Oh dear, that's so worrying. Have you still got your two boys helping you?'

'Yes. We are still trying to track it down. whatever it is.'

'Thank you, Oliver. Keep up the good work. We must be getting on.'

They rode off in silence, for a while Lady Palmer was deep in thought.

'I very much doubt we would have a wolf here,' she said.

Henry had had the same thought and felt there was something not quite right about the Gamekeeper. He didn't know why, but he didn't like him. They cycled on through the woodland until they came to a large and very beautiful lake, among the Pine trees. On the far side of the lake, that Henry estimated would be about half a mile away, there was the boathouse with a little jetty protruding into deeper water.

'What a smashing spot' called out Henry, as he stopped his bike to gaze across the lake. 'Is this all yours?' He asked in astonishment.

'Yes, of course. Our estate stretches for about 7 miles that way.' She said, pointing east. 'And probably six that way; nine or so in that direction; and maybe 12 or so that way.'

'Wow said Henry, what a lot of land.'

'Yes, it is rather. Do you know, this particular spot is one of our favourites?

'Our?' Asked Henry.

'Yes. My husband and I, Lord Palmer. We both agreed that it was the most beautiful place on the whole estate.' She sighed, and then continued. 'The fact that you find it captivating too tells me something about you, yes you have an eye for beauty. Perhaps you will be an artist later in life.'

Henry didn't imagine so, he wasn't much into painting, but then he asked,

'Is Lord Palmer away at the moment? Only I….'

'Yes. He is away,' she interrupted. 'He is in France, behind enemy lines,' and then added. 'Come on let's get going. We have a meeting today, remember?'

They rode on in silence until they came to the other side of the lake, close to the boathouse. Pointing to a large mound, with a staircase leading down to an oak door, Henry asked,

'What's that?'

'Oh, that's our ice house' she said.

'Ice house?'

'Yes. Have you not seen one before?' Henry shook his head. 'Well let me explain, I won't open it up now, but what it is, is a large underground sort of cave, quite large inside, and we use it for cold storage. When the lake freezes over in the winter, we cut blocks of ice from it and put them in the store here. When we slaughter our livestock; sheep; deer; cattle etc, we store the meat in there and it is kept almost frozen all year round, clever isn't it? Come on now, we're almost home.' They could see the house at the top of the hill.

'Right. You go and wash up, and I will see you in the drawing room in 15 minutes time, for the meeting. We will do the stables this afternoon.'

'Yes ma'am.' Henry said 'Thank you very much for showing me your estate, is that what it's called?'

'Yes, that's right. Run along now.'

'He seems like a nice boy,' she thought, 'and what good manners he has.' With those thoughts in mind, she went off to get ready for the meeting.

Henry arrived outside the drawing room, just as George was about to knock on the door.

'Hello Henry, how are you?' He asked.

'I'm fine thank you. How's Mary?'

'She was a bit tearful this morning, but she will get used to it, I suppose. You will come and see her when you can, won't you?'

'Yes. You know I will,' answered Henry.

'Come in,' called Lady Palmer, in answer to George's knock. 'Good afternoon, gentlemen.'

'Good afternoon ma'am.' They replied

'Won't you be seated?' she said. Once they were all seated, she turned to George and said, 'Now suppose you tell me what this is all about, and please, I want to know everything. Everything, do you hear?'

It took George an hour and forty-five minutes, with no interruptions at all from Lady Palmer, to explain all he could about Henry. After a long silence, she said,

'And just when did Shep become Henry's dog?'

Both George and Henry looked at each other in complete surprise.

'When do you think it was, George?' She asked again.

'Well, from the moment that Shep found him in the park keeper's shed I suppose.'

'And that was the morning after I came to the school to pick up Kate?'

'Yes,' said Henry.

'Now tell me, George, who else knows about this boy's incredible life.?'

George took a deep breath and said,

'My wife Mary, the Prime Minister and his Secretary.'

'That's all?'

'Yes. That's all. Well you now too, of course.'

'And what about Kate?' She asked.

'No, she doesn't know,' interrupted Henry,

'And I don't want her to, or she will think I'm strange or something.'

'Well. you are a bit different, Henry my boy,' said George. 'But not strange, no, not strange.'

'Keep it to yourself if you can' said Lady Palmer, but Katie is a very smart girl, you know. Now as for myself, I can't begin to imagine just how all this has come about, but what an asset you are proving to be to our country, and its struggle against these German aggressors. But Henry, a word of warning. If, as you told the P.M. you do really know the secret hiding place of all our country's artworks and treasure, you must be very careful. Watch your back, at all times. While you are here, you are to work with the agent-in - training, in the other part of the house. George is your immediate boss and you must obey his instructions at all times. Never, under any circumstances, can you bring any of your work or problems back here into the West Wing. From now on, you must forget that I am yours and George's superior. I am just the lady of the house and you are my evacuee. Now run along outside and take your dog for a walk. I will see you again in half an hour and we will have some lunch, after which I will show you the horses.' When Henry had left, she said, 'do you know, I knew there was something different about that boy when I was showing him around this morning.'

'What do you mean?' asked George.

'Well, when we got to the deer park, they didn't seem to be at all nervous of him.'

'Yes,' said George. 'I have noticed that he does seem to have a way with animals.'

'I wonder just how he will get on with my horses this afternoon? Well, goodbye George. Thank you.'

They had finished their lunch and Henry sat at the table with a ponderous look on his face, then he said,

'I know who it is!'

'You know who, who is?' Asked Lady P.

'The lady you remind me of,' said Henry.

'And who would that be?

'Janet Keppel, the lady on Eggheads'

'Whatever is Eggheads?' Asked Lady P.

'It's a television programme my aunt used to watch.'

'I thought we were not going to talk about your past, Kate might well think you are strange if she were to hear that.'

'Yes. I'm sorry.' Said Henry. 'I won't do it again.'

'We must be careful, anyway is she nice?

'Who?'

'This Janet.'

'Oh yes, she's a lovely lady.'

'Come on then, let's go and see the horses.'

She turned away to hide the smile on her face, 'lovely lady is it?' She said to herself.

The stable block was just to one side of the house, a long single-storey building and a cobble-stoned yard that housed 10 stables. It was painted white with green stable doors. The first four had horses in them, the fifth one had its door open, but no horse. We keep only five horses now; the other stables are used as storerooms.

'Oh, hello Ned,' she said as a man emerged from one of the stables. 'Henry, I want you to meet Ned, he's our stable lad.'

'Allo, I 'eard you was a comin,' said Ned. 'Shall I show 'im round ma'am?'

'Yes please, if you will. I must go and talk to Cook for a minute.'

'Okay ma'am, said Ned' and he touched the peak of his cloth cap, covering his silver-grey hair.

'Yes. I know what you are thinking.' Ned said to Henry, as soon as Lady P was out of earshot. 'I started work 'ere when I was just a boy, 52 years ago and her Ladyship still calls me the lad, and I be older than 'er. Right now, this 'ere is Miss Kate's pony, he said. 'She calls her Sterling, on account of the silver colour. This next one is My Beauty, and this fine Chestnut Stallion, his name is Sundown. The fourth one in the block is another jet-black mare called Midnight. Now we use Midnight to pull the Lady's carriage when she goes to church on Sunday. The fifth horse as you can see, is not 'ere, and that is because he is being thoroughly naughty, as 'er Ladyship puts it, and refuses to go into the stable. I don't know why, 'e just won't let anyone near him in the paddock. Let's go see what mood 'e's in. Problem is no one rides 'im anymore not since the master's been gone.'

They turned the corner of the stable block,

'There 'e is look,' the big brown horse in the centre of the paddock was not looking its best after last night's storm.

'He looks a bit fed up'said Henry, 'here boy' he called and banged his hand on the side of the white picket fencing.

'He won't come said Ned, he's getting meaner every day. Well, I must be off. I've got work to do and Lady Palmer will be back shortly, as soon as she's finished with Cook.' He turned and started to walk back to the stable block

'What's his name?' Called out Henry.

'Trouble' he called back and don't you get too close to him.'

As Ned left, Henry tried again to get the horse to come to him. After a little more coaxing, the big brown horse came slowly towards him. Henry put his hand out to stroke his nose just as Lady Palmer came around the corner.

She was just about to call out and warn Henry not to get too close to that bad-tempered horse, when something stopped her and she stood still, watching the remarkable exchange between the horse and the boy. That big horse didn't seem too sure about making friends with this stranger at first, but surprisingly he allowed the boy to pat his forehead. All the while, Henry was talking. His voice soft and low, and then Lady P witnessed something she had never before seen in her life. Henry was now stroking the horse's neck and blowing gently up the horse's nose. After a few seconds the horse was completely relaxed. Henry climbed up and sat on the top rail of the fence with its feet hanging down into the paddock. Lady P looked on in amazement at what she was seeing, it was only yesterday this horse was so bad tempered that he would kick or bite anybody who got near him. 'Should I stop this,' she wondered? 'He could get killed in there, but if I call now will it frighten the horse?' She stayed silent, rooted to the spot, and watched as Henry climbed down into the paddock. The horse was not concerned at all, in fact he seemed to like it. Then Henry moved away from the horse about five paces, turned around and said,

'Come on.'

The horse moved towards him slowly and stopped when he got close enough to get a pat on the neck.

'Let's go for a walk' Henry said, and the horse set off at a brisk pace, walking around in a large circle. When he got back to the starting point, Lady P had come over to the fence. Henry looked at her and said,

'I think I can get him back to the stables now, if you like.'

She nodded in agreement hardly trusting herself to speak. Henry opened the gate and walked out of the paddock.

'Come on,' he said, looking at the horse, 'let's go.'

The horse followed Henry all the way to the stables, Henry walked right inside and the horse followed him.

'Shut the door please ma'am,' he said to Lady P, who had followed them every step of the way. She shut the bottom half of the stable door with both horse and boy inside.

'Are you alright in there?' She asked.

'Yes, he's fine now. Thank you.' Said Henry. 'I think he's glad to be home again.'

Henry came out and as he closed the stable door, the big horse named Trouble, stuck his head out over the top.

'I think he wants you to stroke him, Ma'am.' Said Henry.

Lady P rather carefully put her hand up to stroke her husband's horse.

'Well, what do you know, I think he likes it,' she said. 'Now then, young man. Tell me. Why is it that animals take to you so readily?'

'I'm afraid I don't know, ma'am

'But didn't I see you blowing up that horse's nose?' Asked Lady P?

'Oh yes, well I saw them do that in The Horse Whisperer, a film I went to see. I think it is something that North American Indians did with their wild ponies.'

'Well I do declare,' she said. 'Whatever next? 'Ned,' she called as she saw the stable lad approaching 'What do you think of that?'

Ned stared in amazement when he saw Trouble in his stable.

'How did you get him in there?' He gasped.

'I didn't, Henry did,' she said. 'Now, Ned. I want you to give that horse a good scrubbing and grooming. Henry would you like to help him? You would? Good. The next time I see him I want him looking like the fine proud chestnut stallion I know him to be.'

'Can I go and get Shep, and show him my new friends please?' Asked Henry.

'Your new friends? Oh, you mean the horses. Yes, that's a good idea. You go and get him now, and I can see for myself how they're going to get on. If all goes well, we can make Shep a home of his own in one of these empty stables.'

Henry had tied-up Shep in the shade of the large oak tree, near the front of the house, while he had gone to meet the horses. Shep was not keen on being tied up but Henry had promised to be back soon and said,

'Now, you be a good dog and don't let me down.'

So Shep had waited patiently and was as pleased as punch when Henry returned to untie him.

'You must stay on the lead for now until we see how you react when you meet the horses, so no barking and behave yourself, you hear me?' Henry said.

The dog looked at Henry, put his head on one side and had a look on his face that said 'who me?'

'Come on now, let's go.'

Shep knew they were going to the horses of course; he could smell them on Henry. They reached the stable block where Lady P was waiting expectantly.

'It might be better if you introduce them ma'am, better for the horses I mean, and can you please tell Shep the name of each horse in turn?'

'Oh well, here goes,' she said, as she walked over to the first stable and all five horses turned their heads and watched as Shep trotted alongside Lady P. 'This is Sterling,' she said. 'Sterling, this is Shep.' The horse looked at the dog as if they'd known each other all their lives. Shep sat down outside the door and looked up and sniffed. 'Let's move on Shep, this is My Beauty,' and so they went on, all the way down to the last horse, Trouble. When they were introduced, as it were, instead of sitting down, Shep stood on his hind legs and put his head as close to the horse as he could. Lady P was just about to pull him back down, when Henry said,

'It's alright ma'am, he's just getting a closer look, and you can see Trouble is not worried. Now if you would let him off the lead, maybe we could show you something.'

'Are you sure it's alright?' She queried.

'Yes ma'am.'

'Well, okay then. Here goes.'

She unclipped the lead and patted Shep's head. Henry then said,

'Come here Shep, sit down.' Henry bent down close to Shep and said, 'Which horse is Sundown?'

Lady P watched in amazement as Shep trotted over and sat down outside Sundown's stable.

'Well bless my soul' said Lady P.

'Will you try ma-am?' Henry said.

'Alright,' she said. 'Find midnight for me Shep.'

Which of course, he did.

'I just can't believe it.' She said, as the dog found each horse in turn. Even when Lady P tried to confuse him by changing the order.

'Ned,' she called. 'I want you to make a kennel for Henry's dog Shep, in that empty stable there. Make it nice and comfortable for him, but first get the stallion cleaned up if you would.'

CHAPTER FIFTEEN

Lady P told Kate it was no longer convenient for Henry
to live with George and Mary, and that it had been
decided he should come and live in the west wing with
them. She also told her that he would be going to
school in the east wing of The Grange where he was
going to be given private tuition to prepare him for
college.

'What did Mary think of that?' Kate asked.

'Well, she didn't like it very much, I know it has
come as a bit of a shock to her, losing her evacuee in
this way, but he will be able to go home to them at
weekends, if he wishes. Now I want you to show him
around and give him all the help you can to settle in
here. It will be nice for you to have a friend living here,
won't it? I understand you two get on well, is that
right?'

'Why is he having this private tuition at the
Grange?' Asked Kate.

Lady P was silent for a moment, then said 'Kate my
dear, I want you to listen to what I have to say very
carefully. Henry is a nice boy and he is very clever but
in two subjects he does have the need for special
training, I have made up my mind to see that he gets
it, hence these new arrangements. Now I would rather
you didn't ask me any more questions about it or
Henry for that matter, he is a rather sensitive boy and

you may embarrass him. These are my wishes Kate and I am putting you on your honour to obey them.'

Then her tone softened, and she said,

'Oh dear, it does all sound rather dramatic doesn't it, but I know I can trust you.'

Later, on Monday afternoon, Kate showed Henry around the rest of the west wing.

'Do you like your room?' She asked him.

'Yes, it's cool he said.'

Kate had known him long enough to understand what he meant by cool.

'Mine is too she said, it's the same as yours almost. But I like the colours in mine better. Do you think you will like it here Henry?'

'You must be joking,' he said. 'What's not to like? Swimming and boats on the lake, fishing and horses. Ned's going to give me riding lessons, starting tomorrow.'

'Oh good,' said Kate, 'then you can come riding with me, when you're good enough.'

'Well, we shall see won't we,' said Henry. 'Ned told me that you are very good, a natural he said, and Lady P said you have a very good seat.'

'Did she really? Oh, that's nice of her to say. Do you like her Henry?'

'Yes,' he replied. She seems like a nice lady, and she likes my dog too.'

'Oh, that's good,' said Kate. 'Cook is very nice too. I like her and she'll probably find lots of bones for Shep. There is the housekeeper as well, she is a bit formal but she can be very kind too, and then there's Charles. I don't know what his title is but he seems to do a bit of everything, he is a butler one day and the handyman the next, he drives the pony and trap when Lady P and I go to church. He sometimes has a sour look on his face but he is very comical really and he's always ready to help you if you need him. The only one I don't like here is the gamekeeper.'

'Why don't you like him?' Asked Henry.

'I don't quite know, but there is something sinister about him, I don't see him very much but when I have been out riding Stirling around the lake, I have seen him in the woods once or twice. He always seems to be hiding when I ride by though. Anyway, shall we go and see the horses now? I hear Shep has got a nice new kennel there and Lady P told me that it was you who got Trouble back inside.'

'Yes, that's right. He's looking so good now we have given him a good grooming. What a beautiful chestnut colour he is.'

'What do you mean, WE groomed him?'

'Ned and I,' said Henry.

'I didn't know you knew anything about horses,' said Kate.

'I'm a quick learner' said Henry, as they set off for the stables.

'Come over here said Kate,' she indicated a sheltered spot near the wall of the house, 'I want you to meet my little pet.' She knelt-down and picked up a small tortoise.

'Wow, isn't it tiny?' Said Henry. 'What's its name?'

'His name is Lightning.'

'Is that because he moves so fast?' Laughed Henry.

'Why else?' replied Kate, as she put the little tortoise back in its home. 'I was going to keep a rabbit but I changed my mind when I found that Cook put them on the menu.'

'Really? Do you mean to say..?'

'Yes, we often have rabbit pie and rabbit stew, it's very nice. The gamekeeper brings in half a dozen each week, he shoots them on the estate. I think it's one of the reasons why I don't like him. Do you like pheasant and partridge?'

Henry confessed he didn't know.

'They eat a lot of food like that here, especially when they have a dinner party, and you should see some of the guests that visit here, film stars and royalty.

'Really?'

'Yes. When I first came here, I saw Lord and Lady Mountbatten and I've seen Princess Margaret and Princess Elizabeth. They don't have parties now, not since Lord Palmer left,'

'Oh. He is in France somewhere, isn't he?'

'Yes. Missing, presumed-dead Cook says. It is a worry for her, isn't it?'

'For Lady P you mean?'

'Why yes, of course, and so it is for thousands of wives and children all over Britain that get the same bad news.'

MISSING PRESUMED DEAD

'When will this terrible war ever end? Do you think we will win Henry?

'Yes. I'm sure we will,' he answered. Thinking to himself 'I wish I could.....'

Just at that moment, Shep came bounding up and made a big show of affection towards Kate who he hadn't seen for a while.

'Lady P told me how clever he was, getting to know the horses so quickly. I wasn't surprised, I know just how clever he is. We are so lucky aren't we Henry, to have all this? The best dog in the world for a pet, beautiful horses to ride, a lake for boating and fishing and a wonderful home to live in, it's all so perfect, isn't it?'

'It certainly is. But why are you looking so glum when you talk about all this happiness?'

'Well, you see I can't help thinking of all the other kids that were evacuated with us. How many of those do you think have it as good as us?'

'None, I shouldn't think. I know what you are thinking, some people get billeted with awful people like I did first of all and get treated as slaves almost.' His mind flashed back to Sherwood Road, the first house he was sent to.

'Another thing that worries me is that some children don't get enough to eat. We have one girl at school who brings a sandwich to school each day and its nearly always powdered egg. Sometimes, when she gets home, all she gets for supper is another powdered egg sandwich. The woman she lives with keeps most of the food ration for herself, she is a big fat lady and this poor girl is as thin as a rake. Some of the other girls looked very thin too. I try to take extra lunch to school to help out when I can. Cook used to say *'I don't know where you put it all'* and *'There is a war on you know.'* But she soon realised what I was doing and she had a word with Lady P about it. She said to Cook 'Well I *thought I saw her slipping bits of her meal into her napkin yesterday, so that's what it's all about.'* Anyway, starting next week she's agreed to pay for school dinners for five of the girls, so at least they will get some food.'

'Did she tell you off for taking the food?'

'No. I thought she was going to, but she said 'you should have come straight to me and in future if you have something that is troubling you, you are to come and tell me about it. You know a trouble shared is a trouble halved.'

'I suppose she is right,' Henry observed. 'But of-course, not all the evacuees have got it bad, some boys and girls have finished up in better homes than the ones they left in London, there are a number of slums in poverty in London.'

'I suppose some good will come out of this terrible war, but I just wish it was all over,' said Kate.

'It will be soon, I just know it,' said Henry. 'Come on Kate, ask Shep to pick the horses when you name them.'

'Alright. Show me which horse is Trouble Shep.'

The dog went straight to the stable door of the chestnut stallion, the horse did not flinch as Shep stood on his hind legs with his front paws resting on the top of the door, his head inches from Trouble's nose.

'They seem to be good friends already, and the horse looked so content.'

'Yes, and do you know what?'

'What?

'In 10 days' time. I will be riding him.'

'Oh really?'

'Yep,' he replied confidently.

'It's not like riding a bike you know, and anyway, I know two people who won't let you ride him.'

'Yes? Who are they?'

'Lady P for one.'

'And the other?'

'Trouble. Come on, let me show you the rest of the house.'

They said cheerio to the horses and Shep, and walked back to the house. Ned the stable lad watched them go. 'Just like brother and sister those two,' he said to himself 'nice kids too.' Walking back, Kate stopped, and turning to Henry, said,

'If I tell you something, you won't laugh, will you?'

'If it's a good joke, I will.' He answered. But as soon as he saw the serious look on her face he said 'No, sorry. I won't laugh, I promise.'

'Are you sure?'

'Yes. I'm sure.'

'Okay then' she said. 'I think the house is haunted.'

'Haunted? You're joking aren't you?'

'No, I'm afraid not.'

'What makes you think that?'

'I have seen a ghost.'

'Now you are joking.' Henry said.

'No, I'm serious. I saw the ghost of Molly, down in the cellar. Come with me I want to show you something.'

'Are we going to see a ghost?' He asked, hesitating.

'No not now. Come on, it won't hurt you.'

Cheered up a little by the 'no, not now,' Henry followed Kate back into the house. She walked through and stopped outside the kitchen, there on the wall was an old picture in a frame. A picture of the entire kitchen staff of 1755, each one with their name written below them. The kitchen maids were all dressed in black, with white aprons and hats.

'Now you see this one here,' and Kate pointed to the kitchen maid called Molly.

'Yes,' said Henry. Wondering what he was going to hear next. But at that moment the door to the kitchen opened and Cook poked her head out.

'I thought I heard voices,' she said. Seeing they were both looking at the picture of the old kitchen staff, she said 'Telling you the legend, is she? Well don't you believe a word of it, Henry my boy. She will be showing you bloodstains next. Come on now, the pair of you. I have work to do.'

'Alright,' said Kate, and she noticed Henry looked a little less worried after hearing what Cook had to say. But his expression changed again when Kate said 'You know Cook only says that to make you feel comfortable, but deep down she believes the story too.'

'What story?' He asked.

'Well,' said Kate. 'Let's sit here on the stairs and I will tell you. Have you ever heard of Dick Turpin?

'The famous highwayman?'

'Yes. Well apparently he and Molly the kitchen maid were lovers. One night in 1759, Dick Turpin was running from the law, having pulled off a daring daylight raid on a coach and horses carrying Lord and Lady Barrington, who were on their way home to their country estate in Newbury. 'STAND AND DELIVER' he said as he barred the way, pistols drawn, sitting astride his magnificent horse Black Bess. After robbing them of their money and jewels, including a beautiful bracelet studded with emeralds, he rode off into the woods and made good his escape. That night, after dark, he arrived at The Grange. After hiding Bess in the nearby woods, he climbed the ivy growing on the side of the house until he got to Molly's window, she opened it and let him in.'

'What happened next?' asked Henry.

'Ahem,' said Kate. Apparently, Dick Turpin gave Molly the bracelet, just to try on, but Molly didn't want to take it off.'

'Is that the bracelet with the emeralds in?'

'Yes of course,' said Kate. 'There was an argument and then a fight. Molly started to scream very loudly. Turpin had to stop her, she was waking the whole household. In the struggle, he took his knife and killed her. By this time the men of the house were banging on the door. Dick Turpin made his escape out of the window, ran to his horse, leapt on her back and rode all the way to York, where he was eventually captured and hung.'

'So, they knew it was this Dick Turpin because Molly was still wearing the emerald bracelet when they found her?' Henry queried. 'My, that's some story, but what does that have to do with the ghost?'

'Follow me.' Kate said, and started off up the stairs.

Henry followed, and at the top of the stairs Kate said,

'This is our floor, our rooms are along there and up there,' she said, pointing to the ceiling.

'There?'

'Yes and look here. This stain is Molly's blood and no matter how many times they paint over it, it still shows through.'

Henry stared in amazement, not sure if he could believe the story or not,

'Well, that's some story Kate but you said you had seen a ghost?'

'Yes, I saw Molly's ghost, and that's how I knew it was her blood.'

'Oh, I hoped you were going to say it was Turpin, or maybe his horse.' Henry said with a grin.

'Now you are laughing at me, aren't you,' said Kate?'

Henry could see she was a little upset at his reaction.

'No, I'm not really. But I do feel that Cook may be right when she calls it a load of hogwash.'

'Well,' said an indignant Kate. 'Shall we go into the cellar and check?'

'Okay, let's go.'

'No, not now, it has to be after midnight. That's the time Molly was killed.'

'Alright, we'll do it tonight.' Said Henry, trying to sound brave but Kate could tell he wasn't too sure.

Later that evening, when the rest of the household was sleeping, the two of them made their way down into the cellar.

'Come this way,' said Kate.

'Alright, I'm coming,' said Henry.

'Don't make so much noise, you'll wake everybody up.'

'Not the ghost I hope,' Henry thought.

Kate gently pushed open the cellar door, as quietly as possible and just far enough for the two of them to squeeze through.

'Okay, in you go,' said Kate.

'No, after you,' said Henry. 'You know the way.'

'Alright, chicken. Follow me then.'

Kate went down the cellar steps, switching the light on as she went, it was a large open cellar and off to the left Henry could see a big central-heating boiler. To his right was a door, leading to the wine store.

'Over here, but be careful of the hot pipes,' Kate beckoned to Henry, from her hiding place behind the boiler. Henry joined her behind the boiler and noted that it made quite a noise as it rattled and hummed.

'Where do you see this ghost then?' Henry asked.

'Look on that wall, over there,' Kate said, as she pointed to the dirty-red brick wall opposite. Henry looked but couldn't see anything. 'We have to be patient, she doesn't come out to order you know,' said Kate.

'Well, I think you must've imagined it myself, because if....'

He stopped whatever he was about to say because Kate had grabbed his arm and was pointing at the red wall on the other side of the boiler.

'In the corner,' she whispered.

He strained his eyes but all he could see was a faint white light, that looked like a reflection.

'Doesn't look much like a ghost to me' he started to say. But stopped when he noticed the shadowy light had moved slightly towards the middle of the wall and now you could clearly see, it was the figure of a woman in black. She wore a white apron and looked as if she had a white hat on.

'Oh my gosh,' said Henry as he watched the shadowy ghostlike figure move across the old brick wall. He stood there petrified as he saw it with his own eyes. When the ghost of Molly got to the end of the wall she just faded and disappeared.

'Well. What did you think of that Henry?' Kate asked.

'Wow. That was scary, I don't know what to say.'

'You believe me now, don't you?'

Henry was silent for a while and then he said?

'No, I don't think I do'

'What?' She said.

'Well, I think it's a trick, he replied.'

'What do you mean a trick?'

'I don't know yet but I'm going to find out.'

He was walking round to the front of the boiler and Kate said,

'Don't leave me!'

But Henry could see she had a smile on her face. When he got to the front of the boiler, he had a good look at it and then he said,

'Ha! I see it now.'

'What is it Henry?'

'Well, there is a little glass tube on this temperature gauge and the vibration of the machine is causing it to revolve, and look here, someone has painted a little figure on it and it's working like a projector. As the glass revolves, Molly walks across the room.'

He stood to one side and revolved the glass with his fingers and Molly set off on her walk across the wall. He looked up to see if Kate realised how clever he was. She was laughing all over her face.

'You knew? You knew all the time?'

'Yes, she said.'

'And who was it that painted the figure on the tube?'

'It was me' she admitted.

'Well, what a swizz,' he said. 'What about Dick Turpin and Molly, was that true?'

'No, I made it all up.'

'You little minx,' he said.

'Shush! It's half past twelve. You'll get us into trouble.'

They made their way out of the cellar and Kate said,

'I'll bet that scared you though, didn't it Henry?'

'No, not a bit,' he fibbed. 'I knew it was a trick all along.'

CHAPTER SIXTEEN

Henry started at his new school (the training school) in the east wing of The Grange and, just as with normal school, he was required to attend five days a week. Starting at nine AM and finishing at 4 in the afternoon. Because of the high wall that had been built to separate the west wing from the rest of the house, Henry had to cycle out of the west gate up to the cross road, take a right into the lane and ride almost halfway round the estate before he entered the grounds again, at the east wing. After entering the gate, the driveway up to the house was nearly a mile long. So, the whole journey would take fifteen minutes going and, because of the hill he faced going home, another twenty minutes coming back.

He had been given two days-off to settle in to his new home and so did not start school until Wednesday. On his first morning he was a little concerned as to how he would get past the guards on the gate, but he need not have worried because George was there bright and early to meet him.

'This is the young fellow coming now, I expect .' said the duty officer.

'Yes. That's him,' said George.

'So, you'll take him through will you?' asked the guard.

'Yes. I will,' George affirmed, as he walked over to the bike he had ridden out to the gate. Jumping on he said,

'Come on Henry, follow me.'

When they reached the front steps of the house, George said,

'You can leave your bike over there; they can see it's not an army bike so they won't collect it.' Henry had noticed the one George rode was painted a sort of dirty green like everything else belonging to the army. 'Right, follow me,' said George, and they climbed the steps to the front entrance and entered the house via the Judas gate. Once inside, George said, 'Come in here a moment, this is my office. Right take a seat. Now, first things first.' He produced a small piece of paper and handed it to Henry, it had one word written it, XANADU. 'You are to learn that word off-by-heart, in this office now, and when you have learned it, you are to eat it.'

'Pardon?' said Henry.

'Yes, eat it. It will not hurt you, it's rice paper.'

Henry looked at the first letter and asked,

'Do I pronounce the first letter like an X?'

'No, like a Z.'

'Oh, I get it.' said Henry.

'Do you know it?'

'Yes.'

'And you won't forget it?'

'No.'

'Good, now eat it.'

Henry put the paper into his mouth and when it dissolved, he swallowed it.

'Good. Now that's the password you'll need to get IN and OUT at the gate.'

'Did you just say, OUT at the gate?'

'Yes. We can't be too careful you know. OK Henry, now I will show you around the rest of the house. Most of the rooms are classrooms, language courses are held there, we teach French, German, and whatever else is required. It depends on where a person is going.' George explained.

In one of the classrooms, a desk was covered with a strange assortment of objects; among them was a shaving kit; a packet of French cigarettes; and a box of matches. George pointed to the matches and said

'A magnetic needle runs through the centre of one of those matches, so if an agent needs a compass, he just floats the match in a bowl of water, and it will indicate where magnetic North is.' Next, George picked up the razor and unscrewed the cap from the end, revealing a hypodermic needle in the handle. 'Did you notice the little cap on the end had a left-hand thread, just to confuse Jerry, it's the same with this.' He picked up the shaving brush. 'Unscrew the end here, left-hand thread again, and it reveals a little map drawn onto a piece of silk so that, should it get wet, the map will not be spoiled. Of course, it's dependent upon the whereabouts of the mission.' Also, curled-up inside the handle was what looked like a piece of string, but George explained, 'If you unroll it like this it becomes a piece of paper that you could write a message on.'

'What a pity they haven't invented texting,' thought Henry.

'There are a lot of other hidden things here that you will learn about as we go on,' said George.

On the table, Henry could also see what he thought was a cyanide capsule, but George didn't mention it.

'Right, now we'll go next door.'

The room next door was laid out like a classroom, with rows of chairs facing a large blackboard, either side of which was a table laden with explosives. George explained,

'I am showing you things you won't need Henry, but while you are here you will find out what the agents are required to learn. This, is a one and a quarter pound charge.' He picked up a tin not unlike a tin of corned beef. 'This, is full of high explosives,' and with that he threw it against the wall as hard as he could. Henry ducked, but he had no need, as it was not dangerous until detonated. 'This, is a detonator,' George said holding up a silver tube about 2 inches long, about as thick as a pencil. Also on the table was a roll of safety fuse the same thickness as the detonator. 'This,' he said 'Burns at three feet a minute so if you want to explode this charge you cut a length of this safety fuse, and as you see it fits into the end of the detonator here and you crimp it on with these.' He picked up a little pair of pincers 'Don't do it with your teeth or you might blow your head off. Now, if we cut off say 6 feet of fuse all that's left to do is strap the detonator to the side of the charge, light the fuse, and two minutes later…. BANG! If you need a bigger bang, you can add another one and a quarter pound charge, or seven or eight if you want to, But you still only have to use one detonator.'

'Now we come to this,' he said, and pointed toward what looked like a roll of electric cable, 'This is cortex. Now, if you were to cut a length of this, say about a yard, and wind it around a lamppost or a telegraph pole and then attach a detonator and light the fuse, it would cut the post or the pole in half, or you could do the same with this.' He handed Henry what looked like Plasticine.

'Might I be a proper secret agent one day?' asked Henry.

'No,' said George. The Prime Minister would not allow it, and neither would Lady P, or I, for that matter. The PM wants you here where I can keep an eye on you. Now I think tomorrow you should find out how we recruit agents for training.'

Henry went with George to the little country Post Office, about a mile from The Grange.

'I want us to ride these bicycles.' said George. It was a nice ride along a country lane, very peaceful, and the birds were singing in the trees, it was a beautiful day. 'Here we are,' said George as he dismounted from his bike. 'Bring your bicycle this way, Henry.' He was, by now, pushing his bike round the back of the Post Office so Henry did the same and leant his bike against the wall as George had done. 'We won't be long here, I just have to pick up some mail,' George said as they walked around to the main door at the front of the building. When they pushed the door open there was a loud clanking noise, caused by a bell at the top of it.

'Good morning, George,' said a lady behind the counter. She was wearing an overall with a post office badge that read;

'D Noad - Post Mistress.'

'Good morning, Doris. I've come for the mail.'

'Oh yes, I'm afraid it will be a few minutes yet. We're still sorting,' replied Doris.

'That's alright we're not in a hurry, we can wait. By the way, this is my evacuee.'

'You must be Henry, the footballer,' Doris said with a twinkle in her eye, coming from behind the counter to shake Henry's hand. She was about to say something else when the doorbell clanged. 'Oh, excuse me a minute,' she said, and returned to the counter and asked 'What can I get you sir?'

'Can I have three one and half penny stamps please?'

'Certainly sir,' and opening the large book that contained stamps she took out the three that she needed and said, 'That will be four pence halfpenny please.'

The customer replied,

'I'm afraid I have only got half a crown.'

'That's alright, but I will have to go to the back room and get some change, I won't be long.'

While the post mistress was out the back, Henry was having a good look around the shop. It had all the usual warning signs up on the walls like

CARELESS TALK COSTS LIVES

LOOSE LIPS SINK SHIPS

WALLS HAVE EARS

Henry now had a closer look at the customer waiting for his change, he was a young man in his late teens, wearing a long black overcoat with the collar turned up. He was wearing a black trilby hat with the brim pulled down low across his face. Henry thought he looked a bit shifty and seemed to sense Henry was looking at him, so he averted his gaze. Just then, the postmistress returned with the change and said,

'There you are, all sorted now. Goodbye.'

Turning to George, she said,

'Your mail won't be long now, we had rather a lot this morning, so sorry to keep you waiting so long.'

'It's alright, said George. 'We have plenty of time.'

A few more customers came in for stamps or to send airmail letters overseas, to loved ones in the forces, Henry assumed. Another young man entered wearing a dark coat and hat and glanced over at George and

Henry, then went to the counter and quietly asked for three one and halfpenny stamps.

'There you are,' said the postmistress. 'That will be four pence halfpenny please.'

When the man said he had only got half a crown, the postmistress repeated the procedure as before, going out to the back room to get some change. On receiving his change and stamps the man left the shop. Henry noticed him through the window, cycling off on a bicycle that looked suspiciously like the one George had ridden here on. 'That's funny,' he thought.

'Here's your mail, George. All sorted. Sorry to have kept you so long,' said Doris.

'That's fine,' said George. 'I might send Henry along to pick it up from time to time, now that you know who he is.'

'That will be in order,' she replied.

'Nice to meet you at last Henry,' she said as they left.

Once outside the post office, George said,

'I think we'll walk back shall we Henry?'

'What about the bikes,' asked Henry.

'Don't worry, they'll be okay.'

As they were walking back, Henry thought of the two men at the Post Office and his memory flooded back to his trip to Highworth, and Coleshill, and he told George all about it. When they got back to The Grange, Henry noticed two bicycles leaning against the wall in the same spot as they had been this morning, and they looked to be the same bikes. He looked at George, who had a grin on his face and said,

'I thought that second man took your bicycle but didn't notice what happened with the other one.'

'Yes,' said George. 'I wanted you to see first-hand, how things were done. All new agents starting here must go through the same routine at the post office, and what's more, if they don't produce the correct stamps and change from half a crown, they will not gain entrance to the gates.'

'How clever is that,' thought Henry.

'You may well meet both of those new men in the coming weeks. They both need to brush up on their French. Now let's go in and find some lunch, I'm sure you must be ready for it after that walk.'

CHAPTER SEVENTEEN

Each evening after school, Kate and Henry went to the stables to exercise the horses and for Henry to have riding lessons. The horse he was learning to ride, Sundown, was quite spirited. Henry took to horse riding like a duck to water.

'You gotta show 'im who's boss, straight off,' Ned had told him.

'You're doing awfully well,' Kate said as they trotted side-by-side. 'I can't believe you've only been riding for a week.'

'I find it quite easy really,' replied Henry.

'Good,' said Kate. 'Do you still think you'll be able to ride Trouble in three days' time?'

'No, I said two weeks, didn't I?'

'You said 10 days actually.'

'Well, I'm going to do it anyway.'

What Henry had not told Kate, was that he was having early morning lessons as well as the ones in the evening. Ned had the horse saddled and ready to go every morning by six thirty so that he was back in good time for breakfast with a hearty appetite, and everyone thought he was looking a bit stiff when he walked in.

'Do you think you still want to try and ride Lord Palmers horse on Saturday? Asked Lady P.

'Yes, if I have your permission,' Henry said.

'I will check with Ned, and if he thinks you are good enough, you can do it.'

What she did not disclose was that she had bet Ned half a crown that Trouble would not let him on his back, let alone ride him. That's when Ned had advised Henry to get early morning lessons in. Not unfair after all, ten days is ten days.

Friday evening was Henry's last session and he was now getting Sundown up to a canter,

'Hey, that's good,' called Kate as she followed on Stirling.

She stayed behind for a while then spurred her horse into a gallop and sped past them. Henry was happy with his progress, a canter was quite good, as he was still learning. He watched as she went further ahead, her blonde ponytail bouncing with the rhythm of the horse's gallop.

'She does ride that horse well' thought Henry. 'I'll be happy when I can do that.'

After his ride that evening, he had given the horse a good rubdown and settled him for the night then went along to see Trouble. The big horse backed up a little as Henry opened the stable door and walked in, shutting the door behind him.

'Now then Trouble, you and I are going to have a little talk.' All the time he was talking, he was stroking the horse's neck. 'You have to behave yourself tomorrow, as I'm going to ride you,' Trouble turned his head and looked at Henry. Taking hold of his mane, leading the horse round in a tight circle until he was alongside the drinking trough, still holding the mane, Henry said, 'Now stand still boy, I'm going to climb on your back.' Standing on the side of the trough, he very gingerly slid his left leg over the horse's back. The horse flinched but stayed still, as Henry let go of the other leg. Now he was fully astride the horse and he urged him out into the centre of the stable, letting go of his mane and patting his neck, 'Now then, that's not so bad is it,' said Henry. With that, the horse reared up on its hind legs, his front legs did a cycling motion and Henry slid all the way down the horses back, landing with a thump on his backside in a small pile of straw.

To make matters worse, the horse turned himself around and lowered his head to Henry on the floor with a look in his eye that seemed to say 'What do you think of that then?'

'Why, you bad tempered beast,' said Henry. Hauling himself to his feet, he said 'Come here', before taking the horses mane in his hand again and saying,

'We're going to try again, and this time we will do it my way.'

9 o'clock the next morning, it was a very sore and bruised Henry that led Trouble from his stable. Ready for the big test, he was saddled and ready to go. Catching hold of the bridle, Henry walked down to the paddock. Standing by the fence were Lady P, Kate and Ned. Henry walked the horse through the gate that Ned was holding open, then he saw Cook and the butler hurrying down, anxious not to miss the big event.

'Doesn't he look small beside that big horse,' said Lady P.

'He looks a bit nervous to me;' answered Kate.

'Do you mean Henry or the horse?'

'Both,' Kate said.

'Those trousers he is wearing look a bit tight around the backside,' Cook remarked.

'Yes. They do, don't they,' Kate said and thought to herself 'He looks like he's got a cushion stuffed down there.'

'Do you think he can do this? It looks like it could be dangerous;' said Lady P.

'I'm not at all sure,' said Ned. 'He has had no time at all.'

As he spoke, Henry put his right foot in the stirrup and swung his left leg over the horses back, at the same time grabbing the reins on each side of the head, low down by the horse's mouth. He was barely in the saddle when the horse gave a loud NEIGHHH and reared up on his hind legs, cycling in the air with his front hooves. But this time, Henry was ready and pulled back hard on the reins. Having got the horse under control, Henry trotted to the far-side of the field, turned around, and galloped back to where they were all anxiously waiting.

'That was good Trouble. Let's do it again.'

Once again, they were off, but this time he lifted this hand in the air and shouted,

'Yee Haa!'

After five minutes of galloping, he slowed the horse down to a fast trot and headed to the spot where his audience were clapping. He then turned Trouble around and rode 50 yards out into the field, dismounted and walked to the fence. Once there, he turned towards the horse and whistled. Trouble looked up and came trotting towards Henry, who gave him a lump of sugar and patted him fondly on the nose saying,

'Now you know who is the boss, we can be good friends.'

Lady P was busy talking to Ned,

'That's two shillings I owe you then Ned.'

'No,' said Ned. 'With respect, Ma'am. I think it was half a crown.'

'Oh yes, you may be right. I do think though that having a regular rider again is just what Trouble needs.'

CHAPTER EIGHTEEN

As the months passed, both Kate and Henry spent many happy hours with their horses, and Trouble seemed to look forward to Shep running with them as they rode around the estate. That was just as well, because Shep wasn't going to miss the chance of running through the woods with his four-legged friends.

'Do you know any Morse code?' Kate asked Henry one day.

'Yes, a little.' He said. 'Why do you ask?'

'Well, the girls at school are sending messages to each other by tapping on the desk.'

'Doesn't the teacher hear it? Asked Henry.

'Oh no. You can only do it very quietly, with the girl next to you. Unlike talking, the teacher won't see your lips move.'

'Is it so you can cheat then?' He asked in amazement.

'No, of course not.' She said. 'I just want to know, so we can chat in private.'

'Oh. Okay,' he said 'Do you know what this is?'

He tapped out dot-dot-dot dash-dash-dash dot-dot-dot. Using a light tap for 'dot' and a heavy one for 'dash.'

'That's SOS isn't it? asked Kate. 'Well, everyone knows that.'

'I don't know it all yet, but I am learning, so it will be good to learn together.'

And so they did, talking to each other for an hour each night by tapping the table top.

'It's better than listening to The Archers on the radio, observed Henry.'

After a couple of weeks, the two of them were so good at sending and receiving the code, they used it at every opportunity. Breakfast for example, Kate would send,

'Good morning, can I have your toast today?'

And Henry would come back,

'Yes, if I can have your egg.'

They got so good at it, they just did it naturally and without thinking. One morning, as Henry was asking Kate for her egg, he tapped out the request on the table but did not notice Kate's face, nor did he notice that Lady P had entered the room and was standing behind him. Therefore, he was quite surprised when he heard Lady P saying,

'No, you cannot. Kate needs to eat her own breakfast; she is a growing girl.'

Henry turned around with a startled look on his face and saw Lady P smiling at him.

'You can read Morse?' He said

'I can indeed,' she said 'And if you two want to keep anything from me you had better send your messages in secret code.' But she added 'I must say I think you are both rather clever to have picked it up the way you have, now eat your breakfasts. Kate don't let him eat your egg, you need the vitamins yourself.'

Two days later, Henry said to Kate,

'I've been thinking about what Lady P said, about sending messages in code I mean.'

'She was only joking Henry.'

'Yes. I know she was, but I thought it might be fun if we made up a code.'

'Well, yes I suppose it would be,' said Kate. 'Do you know any codes?'

'I don't, but we could invent our own.'

'Okay then, we'll work on it for a couple of days and see what we can come up with.'

On Saturday morning, after their race around the lake, which Kate won by a short head because her little horse could negotiate a tight bend through the woods much better than Trouble could. Henry just couldn't catch her on the long run-in, even though it was always a close thing.

'Well done Kate, but I'll beat you on Monday.'

'By the way. How did you get on with the code, did you come up with anything?'

'Yes. I have got an idea. How about you?'

'Yes. But it's not very good,' replied Henry.

'Let's have a cup of coffee in the kitchen, after we have stabled the horses, we can swap notes.'

An hour later they were sitting at the kitchen table with the hot drinks and Henry said,

'Right, what have you got?'

'Okay,' said Kate. 'I have come up with this. Tell me what you think.'

PARTRIDGE

	A	B	C	D	E	F	G	H
A	B	C	D	E	F	G	H	I

TURTLE DOVES

		A	B	C	D	E	F	G
A		B	C	D	E	F	G	H	I

FRENCH HENS

			A	B	C	D	E	F
A	B	C	D	E	F	G	H	I

'As you can see in the top illustration, I have moved the top row of letters along one letter and so the letter A is now B, and B is C, and C is D and so on,' said Kate.

'For the Second Code, called Turtle Doves, I have moved the top row along two letters so now the letter A is C, B is D, and C is E etc. In the third code, called French Hens, I have moved along three letters, meaning A is now D, and B is E, and C is F, etc. Each time you move the top row along it becomes a different code. You can move the top row along 12 times and make 12 different codes, each code has its own name. If I sent you a coded message headed French Hens, you would know that I've moved my top row three times. Can you see what I have done, Henry?'

Looking a bit puzzled, Henry said,

'No. Not really.'

'Okay, well here's a clue. How many letters would you have to move your top row along if I sent you a message with the code Gold Rings? The clue is a well-known Christmas song, let me know when you have worked it out.'

'It seems a bit complicated' Henry replied.

'No. It's easy, listen. *On the fourth day of Christmas my true love sent to me, Four Calling Birds*. So, the code is Calling Birds and you move along four letters.'

'Oh yes, I think I've got it!' cried Henry. 'I think that's great.'

'Good,' said Kate. 'Shall we have a little practice then, but what have you come up with?'

'I was thinking of something like that too,' said Henry. 'But it seemed to be too easy to decipher. I was only going to move the letters along one space though. I think if you keep changing how many spaces you move along each message then it's more difficult to break.'

'Well, with my code, you can move along twelve times.'

'So, explain again to me, if I receive a message from you and the letters have moved along three spaces, how am I to know how many spaces you have used?'

'Because,' said Kate. 'The message will be headed FRENCH HENS, for three moves.'

'And if it has been moved six?' Queried Henry.

'Then the message will be headed GEEESE,' she replied.

'So, if you can move along twelve times, have I got to remember all the codes off by heart?'

'No, the clue is in the Christmas song, called *The 12 days of Christmas*. If you know it, you will know how many spaces to move.'

'I get it now! Yes, I think I know the song. So, if you send a message headed GOLD RINGS, I move along five spaces but if the message is coded SWANS, I will move along seven spaces, is that right?'

'Yes, because there were seven swans,' said Kate. 'By Jove, I think you've got it!'

They practised the code at every opportunity, and both became quite good. Henry was not as quick as Kate but then 'she was one smart cookie' thought

Henry. Although he never told her so, she wouldn't have understood.

As luck would have it, the pair discovered they could communicate with each other from room to room by tapping on the radiator. One evening whilst listening to the radio, Henry was tapping on the radiator to the rhythm of the music, and a minute or two later he heard some code being tapped somewhere on the pipes. He listened for a while and the message said,

'Is that you banging on the radiator H?'

He sent his message back,

'Yes, testing communications. How do you hear me?'

'Too loud and too often, now go to bed.'

Discovering by accident that they could communicate from one bedroom to another was very fortunate and the two of them sent all sorts of messages.

'Are you ready yet?' For example.

It served as an alarm clock for Henry,

'Give me a call in the morning please Kate,' he would say. Or, when doing homework, he would ask,

'How do you spell Mississipy?' The answer came back,

'Do you mean Mississippi?'

And it would be followed by,

'Thank you. Over and out.'

But there would come a time when the radiator system would turn out to be a life-saver, in a way neither of them could have predicted.

It came about one afternoon, after Henry had just come from school, and as it happened he was the only one in the house. Cook and the butler had gone to Reading with Lady P for some sort of Red Cross meeting and Kate would not be home for another hour. No sooner had Henry opened his bedroom door, when someone jumped on him from behind, clasping a rough hand across his mouth. The assailant shoved him violently into the room. Henry heard a voice say,

'Give us that bit of rope and we'll tie him up.'

'Oh, there's two of them' thought Henry. Because so far, he had not seen either of his attackers, but as they tied his hands behind his back, he did see their feet. One of them wore heavy leather boots just like the boots the gamekeeper wore. The other man wore very shiny shoes.

'Right, get that blindfold on him,'

'That sounds like the man in the boots' thought Henry.

'Hold him still then,' said the other one, in a rather posh voice.

After they had blindfolded and gagged him, Henry felt them tying his feet together. He was then roughly thrown to the floor and one of them said,

'We can take these masks off now; he can't see us.'

'A good idea,' said the well-spoken one.

Leather Boots then said,

'Now, you sure you can get the car?'

'Yes. Don't worry, I've got the Bentley. It's got a large boot so he'll fit in there alright.'

'Ow much did you 'ave to bung 'em for that?'

'It wasn't cheap; I had to give them £10. But I suppose it won't matter, considering we are going to get £75,000 when we hand him over to the gestapo in the morning.'

'This is going to be in pounds and not those German marks, isn't it?'

'Yes. Of course,' came the reply.

'Where is this U-boat going to come in.' enquired *Boots*.

'It is going to come right up Fareham Creek and it will surface at three forty-five in the morning. We will only have 10 minutes to hand the boy over and get the money, before the tide turns.'

'Ow long will it take us to get to Fareham?'

'About an hour and a half,' said the other man. 'It's less than two hours to Portsmouth from here and Fareham's before that. Right now, the girl will be home from school in 10 minutes and 20 minutes later, she will leave again to catch the bus into town. We can leave him here for now, lock the door, and we can pick him up as soon as she leaves. You drive the car round, and if anyone's about, that car won't raise any suspicions as it's seen here often. Come on let's go.'

'Yeah, but what if she don't go back out?'

'Don't worry, she will. I know she has an appointment at the dentist and then she's being picked up by her ladyship.'

'But if she doesn't, then you'll 'ave to shoot her.'

Henry heard the door close and the key turn in the lock, he lay there trembling on the floor for five or ten minutes wondering just what he was going to do. He managed to get himself into a sitting position and sat there with his hands behind his back; his feet tied together; blindfolded and gagged. 'Not much chance of getting out of this' he thought, 'but wait, what if I could get my hands underneath my bottom and...' he started trying to push his hands down to the bottom of his back and after a great deal of wrestling and a lot of pain, he succeeded in getting his hands under his bottom and down to the back of his knees. Drawing his knees up under his chin, he tried to walk his heels backwards over his hands. But that wasn't going to work because his shoes were stopping him. Now he had another operation to perform, he knew if he could get his shoes off, he could do this thing. Knowing he was leaning against the wall near the radiator, he realised he wasn't far from his bed where there was a bar going between the legs at the foot of the bed. With a great deal of effort, he lifted his legs onto it and prized his shoes from the heels. Once free of his bulky shoes he inched his feet forwards and over his hands. Success at last! He was now sitting on the floor with his legs straight out. He was tied at the ankles and wrists, but his hands were now in front of him, so he was able to lift his blindfold a little.

He sat on the floor and tried to relax after his strenuous effort, and he began to think about his captors. 'Who could they be and how did they know so much about him, and Kate? It was not her usual routine to go out after school, and they are going to sell me to the Germans??? Who knows about me? Let me see; George and Mary; Lady P; the P.M. and I think that's all. It certainly wasn't any of them. Then he thought about the shiny shoes one of his assailants had been wearing. I know who wears shoes like that, and come to think of it, sounded just like him too. It's the PM's secretary! I'll bet he was listening when I said I knew where all the works of art were hidden. Now what was his name? Brian, I think. But what about the other one?' He asked himself.

'My goodness!' he said out loud. 'I know that one too, it's the gamekeeper.'

Just at that moment, his thoughts were interrupted by a knock on the door. 'Oh, that's Kate.' He thought, and tried to call out. But he was still gagged and could not be heard. So, after a moment, Kate moved away and went to her room. Kate was changing out of her school uniform when she heard on the radiator,

'DOT DOT DOT DASH DASH DASH DOT DOT DOT.'

Kate responded,

'Is that you H?'

Then in code, Partridge (the easy one), she received a message telling her that her life was in danger and to leave the house straight away.

'Use the kitchen door. Get help. These men are armed. I am a hostage,' came the message from Henry, with details of the car to be used and the destination, Fareham Creek in Hampshire. 'This is not a hoax,' tapped Henry. 'Please try to get in touch with

George and tell him to bring military police, hurry, leave the house straight away. Your life is in danger.'

With that, she grabbed her purse and ran out of the room. Stopping at Henry's door to show him she got the message and would do what he had instructed. As she left the house, she was unaware of the Bentley hidden in the woodland or of the two men inside that were watching her.

'There she goes now, rushing off to catch a bus, like I said. Now we can drive the car round to the front steps,' said shiny shoes. Who was indeed, as Henry had suspected, Brian, the PM's Secretary. 'I will go and get the boy now, so you can open the boot and be ready to leave as soon as we get him in there.'

Three minutes later, Henry was bundled into the boot of the Bentley. His feet were still tied but at least his hands were in front of him, it was going to be a bumpy ride. Kate was soon at the phone box which was next to the bus stop and was just closing the door to the booth when she noticed a green Bentley drive past at very high speed. She dialled the number which she knew off by heart, having called it many times to speak to Henry in the early days, before he had moved to the Grange. She waited anxiously for it to be answered. 'Oh, please come on, be quick' she said to herself as the receiver was lifted and Mary's voice answered.

'Reading 135.'

'Oh Mary, is George there please?' Asked Kate, relieved to have got a reply. 'It's Kate here and I must speak to him urgently, Henry is in danger.'

'No, I am afraid not. I've just rung his number at work and he didn't answer. But what is the matter and how is Henry in danger?'

'Oh dear, I don't know what to do now. Henry's been kidnapped, Mary.'

'Did you say kidnapped??' Gasped Mary.

'Yes, but now I don't know what to do. Will you ring the police? I'm going to get my bike and try to find Lady P.'

With that, she put the phone down and ran out into the road. It had started to rain so she ran as fast as she could back to the house. Just before she reached the corner, she noticed that a car had slowed down and was now beside her. Hearing a familiar voice call her name she turned and looked inside the car, it was George.

'Oh George, he's been kidnapped! How did you get here so quick?'

'Who's been kidnapped, and what do you mean how did I get here so quick? Get in my dear, you are getting soaked.' Kate got into the passenger seat.

'Right, take a deep breath and tell me what this is all about.'

Two minutes later George slammed the car into gear and hit the accelerator pedal so hard it caused the back wheels to spin in a cloud of smoke, and they were still smoking when he screeched to a halt on the gravel drive at the front steps of the Grange. Kate ran up the steps behind George and when they were outside Henry's room he said to Kate,

'Is this his room?' Kate nodded and noticed George had produced a gun from somewhere. The door was half open when George whispered to Kate, 'Stand back.' He kicked the door open and charged into the room which was of course, empty. George put his gun away and sat down on the bed, deep in thought, after a minute he said, 'Kate, this is what we are going to do. First, I want you to get a pen and paper and while I go down and make some calls. I want you to write down every single word you can remember from the message Henry sent you on the radiator. Think carefully now, every word.'

George returned a few minutes later and Kate was dressed in her warm coat and heavy shoes, she had a bag with some food and drinks in.

'Where are you going?' Asked George, looking her up and down.

'Portsmouth' she said, 'With you.'

'I don't think so, said George.'

'But I know the car,' she said.

'You do?'

'I think I saw it just before I phoned Mary. By the way, did you phone her to tell her you will be late tonight.'

'Kate, whatever am I going to do with you? Of course I phoned her. Alright you can come, but I must warn you now, you are to do everything I say. Do you understand?'

'Yes,' she agreed.

'Right, let's go then.'

They made their way down to George's car.

'Could you pass me that roadmap please Kate?'

'Let's see which is the best route.'

Kate found the roadmap in the glove compartment and said,

'Please can we get started George. They will be getting away.'

'Kate, you must let me do things my way. Try to keep calm, we must use our brains and think of a plan to cover all aspects. They won't leave Henry there to sit on the quayside for hours on end, they'll hole-up somewhere on the way, until the time is right. In the meantime, you and I are going to drive on down to Portsmouth, where we have an appointment with the Navy.'

'Why would the Germans want Henry?' Kate asked. 'I just don't understand it.'

George looked at her and said,

'We had better get on our way now Kate'

'You know why, don't you George?' She asked.

'Alright, yes. I do know. But Henry is going to have to tell you himself, so please don't ask me anymore. You can ask him tomorrow morning, when we've got him back safely.' George started the car and they drove to Portsmouth in silence.

When they reached the naval headquarters, George showed a pass to the sentry on the gate. After he had looked at it and handed it back, he said,

'And the young lady sir?'

'She is with me,' said George.

'I'm afraid she can't come in without a pass, sir.' Said the sentry. 'Just one moment, here comes the officer of the watch.'

George chatted with the officer of the watch for a minute and it was decided that Kate could have a cup of tea in the duty office, while George went in to talk to whoever it was he had come to see. The officer of the watch, Lieutenant Dawson, was a kind young man who told Kate she could have sugar in her tea if she wanted or if she didn't want tea, she could have some 'khi.'

'Khi, what's 'khi?' she asked.

'Well, it's chocolate really. But navy-style.'

'Ooh, yes please.'

'We drink it at sea, keeps us nice and warm during the middle watch. Is that your dad you came with?' He asked.

'No, she said. He's the...' and then added, 'I'm not allowed to say.'

'Quite right Miss,' said Lt. Dawson. 'Careless talk costs lives, and all that.'

'Careless talk' she thought. 'I wonder how poor Henry is getting on?'

Ten minutes later, George came back and said,

'Okay Kate, we can go now.'

They said goodbye to the sentry and both he and Lt. Dawson gave a smart salute. George drove around the corner and stopped outside a building that said, OFFICERS CLUB.

'I have got some passes for us to go in here for a meal but before you get out Kate, you might like to know we are going to have some Royal Marine commandos help us tonight. Now let's go and eat.'

During the meal Kate confessed she was a bit worried about how Lady P would react to this. George assured her that he had spoken to her, to let her know Kate was with him and in safe hands, and that she needn't worry that she would be in trouble when she got home. The time passed agonisingly slowly, but at long last George said,

'Time to go Kate.'

They had a 15-minute drive to get to the spot where the submarine was due to surface. George was about to start the car when a pair of eyes appeared at his window,

'Don't worry Kate, it's alright,' he said, rolling down the window. 'Are we all set?'

'All set sir.' Came the reply from the camouflaged man outside the car. 'The green Bentley has been sighted and my men are all in place.'

'Any sign of the boy?'

'Not yet sir, but we have sighted the periscope from the U-boat so she should surface in,' he looked at his watch. 'About 10 minutes.'

Just then, another man in camouflage and with this face blackened, seemed to appear from nowhere and said,

'We have sighted the boy; they've taken him out of the boot. His hands are tied but not his feet. They are walking him around the car.'

'Is he alright?' called out Kate.

'Yes miss, as far as we can tell he's unharmed.'

'Thank you, Sergeant. Are your frogmen in place? Asked George.

'They are in the water sir.'

'Very good, let's get on with it,' and the two men faded into the night.

Meanwhile, a complaining Henry was being pushed towards the water's edge,

'My legs have gone to sleep.'

'Well keep moving them, you need to get the blood circulating. Come on, get walking around the car.'

All the time he was walking, he was looking round to see if he had any chance of running away, but the gamekeeper had a tight grip on his collar and his legs were not working properly. Anyway, he could see no sign of help anywhere. The U-boat was beginning to surface and suddenly was floating there, right by the jetty. A round hatch opened on the front and out climbed a seaman in a white jersey. He wore a blue beret and carried a sub machine gun. Once clear of the hatchway, another man came out of the opening, carrying a small suitcase. This man had no hat but was wearing a long black leather coat and knee-high leather boots. He stepped up onto the jetty and turned back towards the sub.

'Lights,' he said, at which point a searchlight shone and lit up the 3 figures standing in front of the Bentley. He gave another signal with his arm and the light was turned down low. 'Come forward' he ordered and all three moved toward the man from the S.S.

By this time, George and Kate had parked within sight of the jetty and could see what was going on. George turned to Kate and said,

'Under no circumstances are you to leave this car Kate. I want you to get in the back seat and stay there quietly, do you promise?'

Kate gave her word and George took the handbrake off the car, sending it coasting to the side of the

Bentley. Both cars were in shadow now as the light was concentrated on the two men and the boy. The S.S. man commanded,

'*Put down your veppons.*' The gamekeeper and the secretary both threw down their guns. '*Now bring zuh boy closer,*' he ordered. '*Vott iss your nem?*' Henry just looked at him with a vacant look on his face. '*I vill ask you vun more time, vott iss your nem?*' This time Henry responded, but strangely, he put his head on one side, looked up to the sky, and screwed up his face. He opened his mouth, and pointing to it with his fingers to indicate he couldn't speak, he gurgled,

'*aghg ummre hugggje,*' like a mad demented fool. At the same time, letting the spittle that he had been working up in his mouth, run down his chin. The man from the S.S. took a step back,

'Mein gott!' he exclaimed. 'This boy is a lunatic, Dumkopfs! What are you trying to tell me?'

He backed away towards the U-boat while Henry was still pulling faces and acting like a crazy person. Brian, the Secretary, bent down and picked up his gun. Then everything seemed to happen at once.

The whole area was flooded with light, from a powerful military searchlight, and a voice through a loudhailer ordered,

'Put down your weapons, and put your hands in the air.'

With a rush, the SS man dived into the hatch of the submarine, quickly followed by the man in the white jumper, who pulled the hatch closed. On the jetty, the gamekeeper grabbed Henry by the scruff of the neck and was about to punch him in the face, but soon let go when he felt the pain of Henry's well-aimed kick to the kneecap. This was Henry's chance to run for freedom but as his legs were still cramped from being in the boot of the car, he wasn't moving too fast. He stumbled across the open space to where the two cars were parked, the gamekeeper was now giving chase. Henry got to the cars and ran around the outside of the Bentley but the gamekeeper tried to cut him off, running between the two cars. Kate saw her chance, and opened the back door, catching him full in the face. When he fell to the ground Kate said,

'That's for trying to kidnap my best friend, OK!'

Two commandos pounced on him and said,

'Well done, Miss.'

Just then, George appeared too, giving Henry a helping hand.

'Oh Henry, are you alright?' cried Kate.'

'Yes, I'm alright now. I saw what you just did, that was wicked.'

'Are you going to get in the car now,' asked George?

'Well, I would like to see what is going to happen with that U-Boat first, if I could,' He replied.

'Come on then,' said George. 'You too Kate, if you want to.' They watched as the two assailants were handcuffed and taken away to a waiting vehicle.

When they got to the jetty, the U-boat was nearly submerged with just part of the conning tower showing above the water and going astern as fast as it could.

'They're getting away,' shouted Henry. 'They won't get far, son.' Said a marine officer standing nearby. 'We have had a team of frogmen underwater since we came in and they've attached steel-wire ropes to the propellers, she will come to a stop any minute.'

Come to a stop she did as the wire ropes fouled the propellers and stalled the engine. The submarine came to the surface after a little while. The hatch opened and out climbed the crew with their hands in the air,

'*Ve surrender.*' Said the S.S. man.'

George, Kate and Henry watched as the Germans were led away by four heavily-armed marines. Two others had already bundled the gamekeeper and the secretary into a waiting lorry and headed back to the barracks.

'What will happen to those two? Asked Henry.

'Well,' said George. 'If they are found guilty of selling secrets to the enemy, that is treason for which they could hang, but if it is kidnapping then I'm not really sure. We will leave that to the powers that be. Brian the secretary has been on compassionate leave for a couple of weeks, he said he was looking after his sick mother. So, I'm not sure what he's been up to, or where he has been, during that time. But come on now you two. I think it's time we headed for home.'

'Hang on sir,' said the Marine Sergeant. 'I think the young lad needs those wounds attending to first. We have a medic over here who can look at them if you like.'

Henry's wrist and ankles were red-raw from trying to free himself, during his time in the boot of the car. The medic put some antiseptic cream on and then wrapped a bandage around both his wrists and ankles, predicting he would be back to normal in a couple of days. The officer in charge was talking to George about the Bentley,

'We will arrange to get that back to you in the next few days, we would like to check it over first. In case they have left anything incriminating inside. Are you alright to drive yourself and the youngsters back?'

'Yes, I'm fine. Thank you for all of your help,' said George. Turning towards Kate and Henry he said, 'Jump in now and we'll be on our way.' Once settled in the back of the car and on the way home, Kate said,

'Why would anyone want to kidnap you and sell you to the Germans Henry?'

She looked at him for a reply, but he was fast asleep.

CHAPTER NINETEEN

George was in the office with Lady P, giving her bad news about David Philpot.

'I can't believe it.' She said. After all these months of training and now he has landed in France and broken his leg? How did it happen?'

'His parachute got fouled up in a tree, and as he tried to free himself, he fell 20 feet to the ground. So, we desperately need a new Baker's Boy.'

'Who else have we got?' Asked Lady P.

'No one I'm afraid. Well, no one except Henry, who has volunteered.'

Lady P looked up in surprise.

'Has he indeed?'

'Yes. It came as a surprise to me too,' said George. 'I asked him why he would want to do such a thing and his reply was,

'After learning about the war in his history lessons in school, he wished he'd been there to help in some way. Now that he is here, he feels that his time has come. Also, he thinks that he owes it to the brave young men he has helped to train that have been sent behind enemy lines.'

Lady Palmer was thinking what a great help Henry had been to them, as he was familiar with the French countryside that the agents were operating in and he had been invaluable with the local dialect. He really had an excellent command of the French language.

'But,' she said. 'I just do not think I can agree to someone so young going over there, to such dangerous ground. Plus, he has had no parachute training.'

'Well,' said George. 'I feel the same way, but he has been spending a lot of time with young David and even watched him in training with the parachute instructor.'

'Where is Henry now?' Asked Lady P.

'I believe he is in a meeting with the PM at the moment.'

As he finished speaking, the phone rang. Lady Palmer picked up the red telephone, answered the call with her password, and listened to the voice on the other end of the line. George watched her face drain of colour, then heard her say,

'Very good sir,' and put the phone down.

'What is it?' asked George.

'That was the PM, and he's agreed that Henry can go on the mission. But he is to take Shep with him as he feels that's better than going alone. So, Henry is to be the new Baker's Boy.'

Later that night, Henry and Shep said goodbye to Kate, telling her they would be away for a couple of weeks. Kate had a tear in her eye as she hugged him and told him to take care. After a hug from Lady P, Henry got into George's car for the journey to a small airfield at White Waltham.

'Say goodbye to Mary for me please George.' Said Henry. '

'I will of course, now take good care of yourself. No heroics and take care of your dog,' George replied. Adding, 'Are you frightened Henry?'

'No. Well, I am a little bit. But mainly about the parachute jump.'

Soon after boarding the light aircraft the pilot taxied into the wind and took off. George watched as it disappeared, carrying Henry and Shep into the night sky. There were only two other people on the plane, the pilot and the instructor. It was very cold and noisy. So, when the instructor introduced himself, he had to shout,

'My name is Jim, and the pilot is called Hank, he is American.'

Hank waved to Henry over his shoulder and said hi. Henry introduced himself and Shep.

'You're a bit young for this, aren't you?' Shouted Jim.

Henry smiled and said,

'We hear that a lot. Are those our parachutes?'

'That's right son. Now I know this is your first jump so I'm going to tell you just what to do. You will be fine, so don't worry. It's as easy as falling off a log, just a bit higher! Now, when you hit the ground you need to bend your knees to take the impact, like this,' and he demonstrated. 'Once you are on the ground, roll over on your right or left shoulder like this.' Again, he tried to demonstrate, which was a little difficult in the confined space. Henry tried it and found it quite easy. 'You'll have to explain all that to your dog.' Jim grinned. 'I think you have got the idea, and dogs tend to be okay with parachutes anyway.'

Henry pondered all he had been told, tried the actions again and got the thumbs up from Jim.

'Now, you will go first and Shep will follow. We have a special harness for him there. There are no rip cords to pull because this white ribbon here,' he said, pointing to a white band with a metal hook attached, 'will be hooked onto this bar, unfurling as you leave the plane. Once you are clear, it pulls the rip cord for you, easy as pie.'

Henry patted Shep to let him know all was well. A shout came from Hank to tell Jim they were over France and not long before the drop.

'Right,' said Jim. 'Give me a hand to get Shep into his harness for the parachute. Now, when you land you just need to press this metal tab to release your harness from the parachute.'

'Just like a car seatbelt then,' said Henry.

'If you say so,' said Jim, not knowing what a car seat belt might look like. Shep didn't seem to mind a parachute on his back and sat down quietly once it had been fitted, watching with interest as Jim helped Henry with his.

'Six minutes to the drop zone,' called Hank.

'All ready, back here,' was Jim's reply.

Three minutes later, Jim opened the side door, and the cold night air rushed in.

'One minute,' shouted Hank. 'There's the light, Go-Go-Go and good luck!'

'Come on Shep,' said Henry, leaping out of the plane before he could change his mind.

'Go Shep,' said Jim.

Shep needed no coaxing, as where Henry went, so did he. Henry felt a little tug as the ribbon attached to the plane went tight and pulled the cord to open the 'chute. With that, the headlong rush to earth slowed to a gentle, controlled descent. He looked around and just above him, silhouetted by the moon, he could see the strange shape of an Alsatian dog, hanging from a parachute. Looking down, he saw the tops of trees and was relieved to spot a little clearing that looked ideal for their landing. He hit the ground quite gently, as there was no wind, and his 'chute dropped softly behind him. He quickly undid his harness and was gathering in the parachute when he noticed that Shep had not quite reached the ground. His parachute had been snagged by the branches of a nearby tree, causing Shep to swing back and forth, a few feet from the ground. Henry ran over to help Shep, who was now whining softly. Pulling at the harness to find a release button, Henry heard a voice say,

'Keep that dog quiet, or I will have to shoot him.'

'Mon dieu, it is just a boy!'

Henry turned to find two rough-looking men, both carrying guns. He hoped they were the resistance men he had been expecting to meet so turned to the dog, and patted him gently, saying,

'Quiet now Shep, they are friends.' Before turning back to the men and, in perfect French, asking the men to help release Shep from the tree.

One of the men turned to the other and said,

'So, we have a boy who speaks perfect French and a dog who understands only English. We were not expecting someone as young as you, or a dog.'

'Yes, I know,' began Henry. But he was interrupted by a third person who he had not seen or heard, entering the clearing from the trees.

'It's okay,' the new man said to the others. 'He has been cleared and so has the dog. Get him down from the tree, hide the parachutes, and get them safely to the edge of town. Hurry it will be light soon.'

As they were hiding the parachutes, one of the men said to Henry,

'How many years have you got?'

'Pardon?' asked Henry.

'How many years have you got?' Repeated the man.

'I'm sorry, I don't understand,' said Henry.

'He means how old are you,' said the man. 'But enough talk, let's get going. Keep the dog quiet too.

My men will take you to the edge of the town but after that, you are on your own. Do you have your papers with you?'

'Yes,' said Henry.

'Good, now get going. You have seven kilometres to go, good luck.'

It was almost daylight when they reached the edge of the woods and one of the men took Henry's arm.

'This is as far as we go. Do you see the church tower?' He said, pointing across the field.

'Yes, I see it.'

'Good, now over here is the town square, and there is the boulangerie where you are to stay.'

The second man came out of the trees pushing a rather old and heavy looking bicycle with a small battered old suitcase, strapped to the pannier.

'This is your bicycle; your radio is in the case. Good luck, English boy. The town is full of gestapo, so take great care. Vive la France!'

With that, they turned and disappeared into the trees.

Henry pushed the bicycle along the footpath at the edge of the field, until he reached the narrow road into the town. Once on the road, he jumped on the bike, only to find that he had no gears. The bike had a fixed wheel which made going uphill much harder than Henry was used to, and when he went downhill the only way to rest his legs was to lift his feet off the pedals as they continued to go around.

When they reached the church, Henry stopped to get his bearings. 'Oh yes,' he thought. 'I remember now, down here to the square and then off to the left for the bakery.'

It was quite light now, and one or two vehicles were in the square, some little old Citroen vans, and a horse & cart. Then a convoy of German army lorries rumbled through, on their way out of town. He knew he was getting near to the bakery, because the delicious smell of newly baked bread reached his nostrils, making him realise just how hungry he was. He leaned his bike against the wall of the Boulangerie and telling Shep to wait outside, he walked into the shop. There were two customers waiting to be served, but as soon as the middle-aged lady behind the counter (who he had never met before) saw him, her face lit up with a beaming smile and she said,

   'Enry, how you 'ave changed, I 'ardley recognise you.' She came from behind the counter to give him a hug and a kiss on both cheeks. 'Let me look at you,' she said. Holding him at arms-length.

At that moment, the shop door opened and in came a German officer. The lady looked up and said,

'Bonjour, Lieutenant Schmidt. This is my nephew 'Enry. He has come to live with us for a while. His family were killed during a British air-raid. He is going to help us here at the bakery and will deliver the baguettes to the Chateau. It is too much hard work for my father these days, he is too old to ride that bicycle.'

All of the conversation had been in French, so Henry assumed that the officer was fluent, or at least understood most of it. He must be careful not to slip back into English, he thought.

Lieutenant Schmidt looked Henry up and down before saying sharply in French,

'Papers,'

Henry put his hand inside his coat and took out the new set of IDs that George had given him just before he had left England. The papers had been made to look old and well used, a few dirty finger marks here and there. He passed them to the lieutenant who studied them for a while then gave them back. As he did so, he said,

'I will see you at the Chateau sometime, no doubt.'

Henry's new 'auntie' spoke up and said,

'Yes, the Lieutenant is often on duty in the kitchen, for the early morning delivery. Have you bought me your order for next week?'

'Yes, we will require the same as last week,' he replied, adding, 'Au revoir, madame' as he left the shop.

'He is not so bad, that one,' said one of the customers who had been waiting to get served.

'Bah,' said the other one. 'He is German, that's bad enough.'

When the shop was empty, Henry was ushered into the back room and introduced to the other members of his new family. His new aunt was called Claudette and her father was Pierre, there was also a younger woman called Rosa, who was Claudette's daughter. Henry asked if he could bring in his dog, as he was sure by now Shep would be getting very anxious about him, and very thirsty.

Rosa said,

'Yes, we were told about Shep. Will you bring him to the side door though, not through the shop.' She went with Henry to show him the way. 'Now, you must both be very hungry and thirsty, so we will get you some breakfast before showing you around.'

After a freshly baked croissant; some baked bread; and a large hot chocolate; Henry was shown his bedroom in the attic. It was sparsely furnished but there was a wardrobe and Rosa showed Henry where the radio and transmitter could be hidden within it. He was told he would have an easy day today, so he could catch up on some sleep, after his all-night journey. It wasn't long after laying on the bed that he was fast asleep, with Shep on the floor beside him. He woke in time for the evening meal where he chatted with Pierre, who explained what would happen tomorrow.

Next morning, Henry woke early and was in the kitchen having a light breakfast by five thirty. The first batch of bread had already been baked and was smelling delicious.

‘When you have finished your food,’ said Pierre. ‘We will deliver the bread to the Chateau.’

Outside, Pierre's bicycle was ready. It's wicker basket, laden with 30 baguettes and 12 other assorted loaves, was set in a metal container on the front of the bike.

‘Mon dieu,’ he remarked with a smile, when he saw Henry's old bike. ‘That is a monster. Never mind, you can use mine when you take over in a few days. Now, don't forget Henry. French at all times, and don't appear too inquisitive. But make a mental note of anything strange you may see or hear.’

They pedalled up the slight incline and once past the church they could see the Chateau, dark and foreboding, some 3 kilometres away in the early morning light. Henry could see Grandpa Pierre was quite exhausted by the time they reached the main gate. It was guarded by two soldiers with automatic weapons who scrutinised Henry's papers and searched him for any weapons. Pierre explained to the guards, in his broken German, that Henry would be making the deliveries in future as he was getting too old for the journey.

'Okay Grandad,' said one of the guards. 'We will let the boy in, now we know who he is. That is a fine German Shepherd you have there.' He said, pointing to Shep who had been standing quietly beside Henry's bicycle throughout the exchange. Shep had caught the look in Henry's eye that told him to stay still.

'Alright on you go now,' said the guard.

They passed through the gates and up the driveway to the back door of the Chateau. Henry wasn't sure why but there was something unnerving about the guard who hadn't spoken, something in the way he looked at Henry while his colleague was talking. As they passed the front entrance, Henry was taken aback by the two, 3-metre-long red banners, complete with black swastikas, that adorned the main door. He did his best to hide his reaction though. Mounted over the door was a gleaming bronze statue of a German eagle. Two more soldiers with automatic weapons stood either side of the door. As they peddled on the long driveway Henry looked across the field to his left.

'That's a minefield,' said Pierre. 'All the way to the woods.'

By the back door that led to the kitchen, was a sentry box. Standing inside it was a rather stout German soldier with a machine gun. The soldier stepped out of his sentry box and said,

'It takes three of you to bring my breakfast now, does it?'

Pierre laughed and produced a half baguette filled with salami from the basket. Handing it over, he said,

'Good morning Otto, this is Henry, the new Baker Boy. I am getting too old to pedal up here, so he will take over from me.'

'This is your dog, Henry? The soldier remarked. 'He looks a fine dog indeed, I have one like him back in Hamburg, pity about that floppy ear though.'

Henry looked at Shep and thought, 'I wish people would not keep-on about his ear, I think it's fine.'

He followed Pierre to the kitchen door where they were met by the chef, in a white apron and tall chef's hat. Pierre greeted him,

'Hello Maurice, this is Henry who I told you about last week. He's going to be delivering the bread from now on.'

'Hello Henry, said Maurice. Would you like some coffee?'

'No thank you. Just some water, please.'

As the chef lifted the bread basket and its contents from the front of Pierre's bike he asked,

'Would you like tea or coffee, Pierre?'

'I will have some coffee please, Maurice,'

The chef took the fresh bread into the kitchen and soon returned with the drinks and the empty basket from yesterday. As they drank their drinks, Pierre said,

'We never go inside the kitchen Henry.'

Once back at the bakery, Pierre asked Henry to bring in the empty basket they had bought back from the Chateau.

'Now then Henry. That was all you need to do, to deliver the bread each morning. Do you think you can manage that?'

'I'm sure I can,' said Henry.

'Did you notice that the chef asked me if I wanted tea or coffee?' Enquired Pierre.

'Yes, I did,' said Henry. 'But he only asked me if I wanted coffee.'

'Well, the reason for that is he knows I never drink tea. But if he asks me the question it means there is a message in the basket. So, if you will pass it to me, we can have a look.'

Henry watched in amazement as Pierre unrolled a piece of paper from inside the handle, where it joins the framework of the basket.

'So, you see, here is the message. Now you must take it up to your room and transmit it to your people in London, using morse code.'

Decoded, the message read;

'A new rocket has been developed by the German scientists, in an underground bombproof factory. Its location is as yet unknown. But it's believed to be close to your location. It is being prepared for movement to Calais, where it will be launched and deployed over England, with devastating effect. The weapon is capable of causing more damage than all the previous Luftwaffe raids put together. It will have to cross the bridge at Arras in order to reach the launch site at Calais. Further details will be sent when they are known.'

Henry tapped away, sending the message into the French night, thankful for all the hours of practice he'd had with Kate. That night, Henry lay awake in his bed and thought of all that had happened during the last 48 hours. He began to think very seriously about the enormity of his task ahead, it was all getting a bit scary. 'Well, I suppose I had better get some sleep now,' he thought. Knowing that he had to be up again by Five AM.

Three days later, Henry was ready for his first solo trip to the Chateau. Pierre had loaded the bread into the basket and put it onto the front of his bike.

'You will find this one a lot easier to ride than that old thing of yours,' he said.

Pierre was right, even with all the bread to carry, this bicycle was much easier to handle. He reached the Château with no problem and when the chef greeted him with the question, 'Do you want tea or coffee?' He felt very excited.

Shep bounded alongside him as he pedalled swiftly back to the bakery. Wondering what on earth the latest message would contain.

Meanwhile, back in England. George and Lady P sat discussing the message they just received.

'Good for Henry, he seems to be doing a first-rate job over there, I knew we could depend on him,' said George.

Lady P agreed but said,

'We should pull him out soon though George. His task is almost done, and we really are asking a lot of such a young boy. Even one as capable as Henry. 'Are the commandos ready to retrieve him, when necessary?'

'Yes,' George replied. 'They're on standby, with the local resistance.'

CHAPTER TWENTY

In the days and weeks that followed, Henry was now making all the deliveries on his own. Well, with Shep of course. The dog was always at the boy's side. One morning, as he peddled the well-loaded bike along the drive that led to the kitchen, he noticed that there were rabbits playing in the field to his left. 'That's the field with the mines in,' thought Henry, and he watched Shep rather carefully. He could tell he was only too eager to leap over the railing and give chase, as he did when he was a pup.

'Steady boy,' whispered Henry.

Thinking 'I suppose a rabbit is not heavy enough to set off a mine, but I bet Shep would be.' He shuddered at the thought.

On the opposite side of the road, in the grassy field that fronted the Grand Chateau, was the chestnut mare that Henry was slowly making friends with. Each morning he would bring her a carrot or sometimes a sugar lump. Henry knew he had to be careful and not be seen from the windows at the front of the building, the kitchen door could not be seen though, and that's where the horse would canter to, when the boy and his dog arrived each morning.

The owner of this beautiful beast was General Von Gripp, the senior officer in charge. A tubby little red-faced man with a curling moustache. He wore a monocle that never seemed to leave his left eye. He also carried, at all times, a riding crop. The word was, he was a bad-tempered man and was always trying to find something wrong, except of course with his horse, who he adored.

'Better not let the general see you do that,' said Maurice, as he watched the horse take the carrot from Henry. 'You would be in deep trouble, but come over here, I want to talk to you.'

'I wonder what he wants,' thought Henry, as he walked across the road to where the chef was leaning on the railing, looking out across the minefield. Elbows on the top rail, and right foot casually resting on the lower one. Henry took up a similar pose beside him, waiting for the chef to speak.

Maurice took a deep drag on his cigarette, threw the butt-end over the rail and said,

'Can you see that small white post? Right across the field, on the edge of the forest'

Henry said he could.

'Good, well don't do it now. Wait until I've gone. But you will notice a dab of white paint on this railing we are leaning on, right by your elbow. If you line up that spot of paint with that post yonder, you are looking at a safe path across the minefield. No mines at all. But be careful, it's only one metre wide. I thought you might like to know that. Got to go now, I have work to do.'

With that, he went back to his kitchen, leaving Henry deep in thought. He collected his empty bread basket and set off home, trying to train Shep to run exactly behind him, the dog did not like it one bit. His place was at his master's side and all the way home he wandered out from behind and ran alongside the bike. It was only after three days of persistent training that Shep got to know the meaning of the word 'Trail' and he would follow the back wheel of the bike exactly.

'Good boy Shep. I knew you could do it. But let's hope we never actually have to cross that deadly minefield.'

General Von Gripp rode his horse for an hour every morning, before breakfast. On his return, the horse was usually unsaddled and turned out into the field to graze. But on this particular morning, the General gave instructions to his groom to leave her saddled.

'I may need her again in about fifteen minutes. Just let her run in the field in the meantime.'

Henry made his Baker's Boy run as usual, as the sun was rising above the treetops on a beautiful spring morning. The birds were singing and the air was fresh. It had all the makings of a wonderful day. As he peddled around the drive, he noticed the general's horse was saddled and ready to go. 'That's funny' he thought. 'I wonder why?'

'Morning Otto' he called, as he passed the sentry box.

'He can't hear you son, he's dead.' Maurice whispered to him, as he appeared from behind the sentry box. 'Take this and go, quickly!' He said, hanging a small satchel around Henry's neck. 'Your cover has been blown; you must get away now. Go across the minefield, into the forest and head south. The resistance will try to pick you up. I will join you in two days. Now go-go-go!'

Henry seemed rooted to the spot, until Maurice gave him a hefty kick up the backside that sent him sprawling towards the railing they had leaned on previously. 'But wait, I've got an idea,' he thought, as he ran to the other side of the road where the general's horse was saddled and waiting. He leapt into the saddle and rode out into the middle of the field, just as he saw the armed guards taking aim, but now he was facing the road again and he put the horse at a full gallop. Up and over the first fence they sailed, three strides more and it was up and over the second fence, onto the minefield trail. He shouted to Shep and the dog heard the order tearing under the bottom bar of the railings, to follow exactly where the horse went. Amazingly, no more shots were fired. 'Probably frightened of hitting the horse,' he guessed. 'Anyway, let's slow down a little and concentrate on the little white post ahead.

'Come on' he said to the horse. 'Thirty yards more and we will be clear.' The few seconds that it took to reach the winning post, as he had called it in his mind, seemed to take forever. But at last, they were across and into the safety of the forest.

At first, they picked their way through and around trees, and very thick undergrowth. There was no visible path or trail, and they made very slow progress., All the twisting, turning, and doubling back they were doing was making for very slow-going. Suddenly though, they burst through the trees and into a small clearing. Here they crossed a trail running from north to south and Henry chose the southern route, as he had been instructed. He sent Shep on ahead, who was only too pleased to be freed from his trailing duty and shot off down the track, with the horse and boy following at speed.

The going was much better now and they were making good time, but after forty minutes Henry slowed the pace down to a trot and then a walk. Soon they came to a small stream where the water was clear and looked good to drink.

'We'd better take a short rest here,' Henry told his two companions. But only Shep looked as if he understood. 'Perhaps I should have told you in

German,' he said to the mare. The horse looked up but made no comment. Ten minutes later, they moved on, still following the trail in a general southerly direction. Presently, they came across another stream, or maybe it was the same one they'd stopped at earlier. Henry couldn't be sure. They walked in the sandy-bottomed stream for about a mile and then crossed to the other side, back into the forest. By this time, it was about four in the afternoon and as they had been going all day, Henry was starving.

A small clearing in the forest seemed like a good place to stop. Henry decided it was as good as anywhere and dismounted, trying to rub the circulation back into his buttocks.

'We can go no further today. Let's stop here under these trees and get that saddle off' he said, after tethering the chestnut mare to a strong looking oak branch. As he unbuckled it and lifted it from the mare's back, he noticed what a fancy thing it was. All in shiny black leather, with two very neat saddle bags attached, adorned with silver thread. But best of all, there was a rolled-up military blanket behind the saddle. As he prepared to relax, he began to wonder what was in the haversack that Maurice had thrust upon him as he made his getaway. He took it from his back, sat down on the grass under the tree, and began to investigate. The first thing he pulled out was an army-style billycan. He smiled to himself as he discovered it was crammed with eight plump sausages.

Next was a small pack of dry biscuits; a cigarette lighter; and a little rubber tube full of petrol, for refilling the lighter. Last, but not least, there was a tin that housed a large Swiss-Army Knife with a very sharp blade; a roll of fishing line; and some fish hooks.

'Let's get a fire going Shep. Help me gather some sticks.'

Shep seemed bemused at this suggestion, no doubt he'd have been happy to have his sausages raw! It wasn't long before Henry had a nice little fire going, and some fat pork sausages sizzling in the billycan. While he waited for them to cook, Henry started to pack away the things from the haversack, and it was then he noticed a piece of folded paper, tucked inside the pocket lining. 'What's this?' he wondered, as he unfolded the sheet of paper. On one side he discovered a hastily drawn map in pencil, what the map represented, he had no idea. He turned the page over, and discovered what appeared to be a coded message, but he hadn't the foggiest idea how to read it. It was so jumbled up, but maybe….

***

Just how long he slept, he didn't know. But Henry woke suddenly and was aware that Shep's hackles were up, and he was starting to growl. The horse too was spooked, and was on her feet.

'What's wrong Shep?' asked Henry.

The fire was low but still burning, so he grabbed some more wood to throw on it, his eyes darting about, trying to see what had scared them. His gaze was met by two pairs of piercing green eyes.

Staring at them from the edge of the clearing, were two mangy but savage-looking wolves. Henry picked up a piece of the burning wood, and tossed it in the direction of the wolves. They backed off for a while but soon reappeared. 'I wish I had a gun,' thought Henry, and then he remembered the knife in the haversack. 'They don't like the fire,' he thought. 'I think I know what might really scare them.'

He searched in the haversack for the lighter fuel & the swiss-army knife. The two ugly wolves were getting closer now, crouching low on the ground & growling. Henry hastily cut the top off the little tube of petrol & flicked on the lighter, the wolves stopped again & with a quick squeeze of the tube it ignited like a miniature flame thrower, shooting two great streaks of flame across the clearing. Henry caught one of the beasts in the eye & the other on the head, setting it's fur alight. With loud yelps & squeals, they tore off, back into the woods.

The incident with the wolves left him in no mood to sleep so he decided he would move as soon as it got light. After checking on Shep, he realised that the horse had bolted during the flame throwing episode. 'Great, now that means I have to walk. I hope the horse is OK though. Anything could have happened to her, tearing off in a fright like that,' thought Henry. 'Well, I won't carry the saddle with me, but I had better check the saddle-bags before I leave.' Opening the first one, he discovered a large amount of Reichsmarks, but the odd thing was they all had the same serial number. 'Well, they can't be genuine' he thought. Looking in the second one, he found a bundle of large denomination Francs. 'They could well come in handy, but I wonder what crooked deal Von Gripp was going to make with this amount of money?' Pocketing the francs, he continued his search and was delighted to find a small compass among other bits & pieces. 'What a result!' He said out loud. Shep gave him a quizzical look and continued to hope for the discovery of some food.

Taking a closer look at the piece of paper from Maurice's haversack he could see in which direction he had to go for the village of La Hutte, which he remembered was between Alencon & Le Mans. 'That rings a bell from one of our camping trips I think.' He thought to himself. Maurice had written that he would meet him there at the Café du Paris within three days. Having stopped at the stream for a drink, they found some nice juicy blackberries to eat. While stroking Shep on the head with his blackberry coated hands, Henry noticed he had changed the colour of his coat. 'Now that's an idea! If anyone was looking for a boy with a brown & white dog, they will now see a brown

& black one instead.' After covering the white fur with blackberry juice the pair went on their way.

Coming out of the forest onto a country road, Henry spotted a signpost which indicated it was 3 kilometres downhill to the village of La Hutte, his destination. The early spring sunshine was taking the chill out of the air and they were making good progress. But out of nowhere, Shep darted ahead to where an old man was sat on the opposite side of the road, his bicycle on its side. When Henry reached him, he could see the bicycle was laden with strings of onions.

'Are you alright?' Henry asked, in fluent French.

'Oh yes, 'I am just taking a rest. Pushing my bicycle with all those onions up this hill, & then riding another ten kilometres to the market, is getting too much for me, but I have to do it as we need the money.' As he listened to the weary man, a plan formed in Henry's mind.

'How much will you make if you sell all of your onions today?'

'Well, I would be very lucky to sell them all for ten francs. Things are very up and down these days,' replied the old man.

'That does not sound a lot for all the hard work involved. How much do you think your bike is worth?'

'Not much, there are plenty of old bicycles for sale in the village, but why are you asking all these questions, my boy?'

Henry wondered if he could trust the old man, but decided he didn't have much choice. 'Well, I would like to buy your bike & your onions & will give you forty francs for them, will you agree?'

The old man was surprised at Henry's offer and wasn't sure if he was joking or not, but when he saw the two twenty-franc notes Henry took from his pocket he couldn't believe his luck. 'You have a deal!' he said, reaching for the notes.

'One more thing,' said Henry. 'Will you give me your beret as well please?'

'I will not ask you why you do this crazy thing' said the old man 'but you are welcome to my beret.'

Five minutes later, Henry & Shep set off down the hill towards the village, leaving the old man scratching his head & wondering whether he was dreaming. It wasn't long before they came to the Café du Paris which had a number of tables & chairs setup on the roadside. Sitting close to the road, were a group of German Officers drinking coffee & schnapps, enjoying the morning sunshine. Henry parked his bicycle near the wall, leaving Shep to guard it, and made his way to a nearby chair. When the waiter came to take his order of a coffee & croissant, he said in a low voice.

'I would not sit there; it could be bad for your health. There is space over there with the man in the red beret.'

Henry looked round & saw the man beckoning him. As he got up to move, two of the officers looked in his direction, but soon returned to their coffee. Henry joined the stranger with the red beret & black moustache who said;

'Your dog looks a little older.' Henry was taken aback by this remark & took another look at the man. He realised it was Maurice!

The waiter returned to their table, just as a bell sounded loudly inside the bar. Within seconds, an old grey Citroen van with canvas sides drove slowly past. The canvas was lifted & two men with machine guns strafed the table where the Germans were sitting, killing them all. Before Henry could fully comprehend what was happening, they were speeding off into the distance.

Henry and Maurice made a quick getaway from the café, to the sound of police sirens, whistles and general panic. Henry pushed the bike, loaded with onions, as fast as he could. All the while, trying to look as calm and as innocent as he could manage in the circumstances. Maurice strode quickly by his side and whispered.

'Meet me tonight, in the Bar Tabac. It's just along that road there.' With that, he took off on his own down a small side street.

Shep and Henry watched him go, and then turned left into the road leading to the bar that was tonight's meeting place. The road was downhill, so Henry jumped on the bike;

'Let's get going Shep, time to stretch your legs.'

It seemed like no time at all before the Bar Tabac appeared at the bottom of the hill. 'Might as well pull in there and have a look at the place,' he thought. He pulled across the road to the front of the bar and just-too-late, he saw the French police van pull up outside at the same time. 'Keep calm,' he thought, as he leaned his bike against the wall of the building, as far away from the police as he could. Two very big Gendarmes had jumped out of the van and were walking menacingly towards him. 'Oh God, here we go' thought Henry, as he took his bicycle pump and pretended to pump up the rear tyre. Looking up only when he saw the shadow of the two policemen beside him.

'Have you got a puncture?'

'No. It's a bit soft, that's all.' He replied, as nonchalantly as he could.

'You look a little young to be a trader. How long have you been doing this?' the second officer asked.

'Oh, it's my first time alone. You see, my poor old Papa had a heart attack last week and I am trying to make some money for our family.'

'So, you are going to the street market down the road are you?'

'That's right,' Henry answered. Having no idea if there was one or not.

'So, how much are you selling your onions for?'

The situation was about to get out of hand, because Henry had not the foggiest idea how much onions were worth. But thinking quickly, he said.

'Mother said to get the best price I can.'

'Well, I tell you what, I have just come from the market and they wanted twenty-five centime for a string, and they were not as good as these.'

'Ok, do you want to buy a string for twenty?'

'Sold, said the policeman with a smile. ' He took his string and paid with a twenty-five centime coin.

'Oh, I don't have any change yet officer,' said Henry.

'That's alright son, keep the change. I hope the old man gets better soon.'

Later that morning, Henry sold all his onions to a market trader at a knockdown price, keeping one string around his neck for himself. Now he had some small coins and notes he felt more able to shop for essentials. He bought meat, cheese, bread and two large potatoes. He also bought a large iron cook pot & some cutlery. He lashed the pot on to the back of the bike with most of the food he had just purchased, the rest he stuffed into his haversack.

Henry had noticed that the road he had cycled down on his way to market was close to the woods. He headed back up the road toward the bar, and when it came into view, he began to look for a suitable opening or gap in the trees, somewhere he could hole up for a few hours, before meeting Maurice. He didn't have to go too far before the ideal spot presented itself, a shady little nook by a stream.

'What could be better Shep?' He asked his pal, who of course didn't answer.

Leaning the bike against a tree, he looked around for a suitable place to build the fire, and there right by his feet was a ring of stones blackened with soot from a previous camper. One hour later there was a nice little fire going and Henry had cut three stout sticks and formed them into a tripod over the flames. The iron cook pot was dangling from the centre, containing half the meat chopped up small; one large onion; and one diced potato; topped up with water from the stream. The whole concoction was starting to simmer nicely, and while he waited for his meal to cook, he scouted around to check that he would be alright here for the night. He was feeling very hungry now, so he dipped his spoon into the pot and brought out a piece of meat. It was hot, hot, hot! But after blowing on it for a while, he slowly got to taste it.

'Hey, that's not bad,' he told Shep. But Shep knew already, as he had opted to have his raw.

Next, Henry fished out some potato and then dipped his big chunk of bread in the soup, it really was good. For some reason, and he had no idea why, he was thinking 'I wonder what aunt Maddie would have made of his stew.' He sat there thinking and trying to make sense of this crazy situation he found himself in. Shep, sensing that all was not well with his master, came and curled-up by his side.

'Well, at least I've got you Shep,' he said, stroking the dog.

'What would I do without you, eh?'

CHAPTER TWENTY-ONE

Henry awoke with a start. The time was passing, it was nearly dark and the fire had gone out. The stew pot was still hanging by the tripod over the cold embers. He unhooked the pot still half-full of meat and potatoes, put the lid on and then placed it high up in the fork of a tree.

'Come on Shep, time to meet Maurice,'

Back on the trail, they picked their way through the woods until they reached the road. The Bar Tabac was half a mile away, on the brow of the hill.

'Stay here and wait for me,' he told Shep, and stepped out into the road.

It was very quiet, no traffic at all. When he was about half way to the bar, Henry could see what looked like a person walking towards him. As he got closer, Henry could see it was an old tramp in a long black overcoat. He had a scruffy beard and carried a sort of kitbag over his shoulder. The distance between them had closed to about four or five yards when Henry caught the most awful smell coming from this vagabond. Henry held his nose and gave the tramp a wide berth, but to his surprise the tramp said,

'Stop pulling that face and show me where you are camped.'

It was Maurice!

'For God's sake, what is that smell?'

'When we get off of this road, I'll ditch it.'

'Well, ditch it now. We go into the woods here.'

'Ok,' he said, as he shook it off from his shoulders and let it fall into the ditch that ran alongside the road.

'Wow, that's better,' Henry told him. 'Now follow me.'

'Where's Shep?' Maurice asked.

'He's leading the way up front.'

'Oh, I didn't see him.'

'No, you wouldn't. I don't suppose he liked the smell of you. Whatever is it?' Henry asked, warmly.

'It is skunk, or it was. It's on the coat, it will soon wear off I hope.'

'I hope so too, I have never smelled anything like that in my life. Anyway, here we are,' he said, as they came to the little clearing by the stream, where he had built his fire and cooked his dinner. The shear legs were still in place, but the fire was out.

'Did you do that Henry?'

'Yep'

'Got anything left?'

'Would sir like wild goat stew with potatoes and onions, with a French bread dip. Or..'

'Don't fun with me Henry, I'm starving. I tried to get something to eat at the bar, but they wouldn't let me in.

'Well now, who could blame them smelling like that! Help me light the fire.'

Soon the fire was burning brightly, and Maurice watched in wonder as Henry reached up into the fork of the tree and reclaimed the old stew pot. Ten minutes later, Maurice was eating his stew. Not saying a word, just eating.

'I suppose he must like it, he's eating it all,' thought Henry.

At last Maurice spoke.

'Henry,' he said, 'I have cooked for high-ranking German officers, even Gestapo Generals. I have cooked for British soldiers, and in my country home I have cooked for English gentry. But I have never enjoyed a meal as good as that.'

'Wow' said Henry; I don't know what to say.'

'Don't say anything at the moment; I have something important to tell you. Do you know a man named Peter Schmidt? He goes by the name Smith in England, of course.'

'No, I can't say that I do, but then again I don't know many people in today's England.' As he spoke, he put his hand over his mouth as if to stop the words coming out. He knew he had said too much.

'What I mean is ...'

'Don't worry son, I know who you are. I had to find out certain facts you see, when I was informed that Peter Smith was after you, he knows all about you too.'

'Who the hell is this man,' wondered Henry?

'Well now, I'm going to tell you. When you first met him, he wore smart pinstripe trousers and black shiny patent leather shoes. The second time was when he tried to sell you to the Germans. Yes, that's right, the PMs Secretary. The Germans somehow managed to spring him from jail, and now I hear he is hot on your trail, here in France. It is my job to get you out, and back home. Now, we have four days to keep ourselves hidden. We are going to live in the woods and must not be seen on the road at all. We have about sixty miles to go, but I think we can do it all under the cover of the woods. Most of it anyway.'

Henry sat silent for a while, deep in thought. 'How did he know..? What did he mean? How can this be?'

Maurice broke the silence, 'There is something you should know, about me.'

CHAPTER TWENTY-TWO

'Well,' said Maurice. I know quite a lot about you, so I think it's only fair that you should know something about me.'

'And that is?'

'Well first, let me tell you that my name is Palmer, Lord Palmer of Berkshire. Yes, that's right, you have been living in my house in England and even riding my horse, I hear.'

Henry sat with his mouth wide open in astonishment.

'You mean you are the owner of the estate where I lived, and Lady Palmer is ...?.' Maurice nodded. 'But they told me you were lost in action, presumed dead.'

'Well yes, that's right. The powers that be thought it best, so that's how it is. But right now though Henry, both you and I are on the run. The Gestapo are desperate to capture you because of your insight, or whatever you care to call it. They want you to tell them how to win the war.'

'I can't do that,' said Henry. 'The war has already been won, and not by the Germans. That can't be changed, I can't alter history.'

'I see,' said Maurice, although he did not see at all. So, after a few minutes silence, he said, 'Henry, consider this. You have come to us from a far later time in history, with the knowledge you gained at school, learning all about this war with Hitler's Germany. Did you at any time read about a boy called Henry?'

'Well no, of course not. Because I wasn't here.'

'But you are here, and people will not read about you in history books, because you are to be kept secret, on the orders of the PM. Herr Schmidt and the Gestapo are on our trail at this very moment, they all want you kept very secret, So you see Henry. Perhaps you are to be born again, later in history.'

'Oh, for goodness' sake, Maurice. Leave it out, you are doing my head in.'

'Doing your head in? What on earth does that mean?' Said a puzzled Maurice.

'Never mind, it's just an expression. More importantly, just how do you plan on getting me home?'

'We have four and a bit days to get ourselves up to a small place called St Marie du Pont, it's on the way to Cherbourg. So, we must travel through the woods, as far as we can. We cannot risk being seen on the road. We'd better get some sleep now; we'll start out first thing in the morning.'

At 5am it was starting to get light. Maurice was on his feet and had begun packing his gear back into his kit bag.

'Are you fit Henry?' he asked.

'Yes, I guess so. Let's get going,' the sleepy boy replied.

They set off, leaving Henry's bike and the heavy cook pot behind, hidden deep in the bushes. With Shep leading the way, they headed north on a narrow trail through the dense woodland. After a couple of hours, it was good and light, and they found a stream where they stopped to drink and share the last of the bread that was left from the night before.

'We are going to have to find a way to feed ourselves today,' Maurice said, as he sat eating his bread.

'How, have you got anything in mind?'

'Yes, I do,' Maurice said, 'But that plan will take a day or two to put in to action. In the meantime, we'll need to catch some fish from that brook. While I collect and cut some wood, could you see if you can catch us something for supper, Henry?'

'How would I do that?' Henry asked

'What do you mean?'

'I don't know how to catch fish; I've never done it before.'

Maurice stared at him in disbelief, 'You mean to tell me that a boy of your age has never been fishing?'

'No, never.'

'Oh dear. OK. Do you remember there was some fishing line and hooks in the haversack? Get them out now, and then dig into the bank for a couple of worms.'

Ten minutes later, Maurice had taught him how to tie on a hook, to bait it with a worm, and how to land a big fat rainbow trout.

'Now, take him away from the bank, unhook him and stun him, like this.' Explained Maurice; giving the fish a whack on the head. 'I am going to gather that wood now, you see if you can catch some more fish.'

After about forty minutes, Maurice returned carrying a bundle of sticks, and was delighted to find Henry had caught three more good size fish.

'Wow, that's not bad for a beginner. We're going to eat well today. If you start a fire, I will fillet the trout.'

'Sounds good to me.' Agreed Henry, and promptly set to work. Maurice expertly filleted the fish and cooked it over the fire Henry had built.

'So,' Henry started. 'What is this plan of yours, to get us some more food?'

'Well, you see that long branch resting over there?

'Yes,' Henry said. I noticed it earlier, it's lovely and straight. Must be about six feet long too. Where did you find it?

'I cut it from a yew tree, while you were fishing, so I could make a bow for hunting. I'm going to need some of your fishing line for a bow string. Do you have much left?'

'Yes, plenty. Help yourself, it's in the haversack.'

Maurice cut himself about four meters of fishing line, and twined several lengths together to make one thick bow string, with a loop at each end that slipped neatly into notches he had cut at each end of his bow. He tested it for tension by pulling back on the string and shooting an imaginary arrow.

'I guess that will do,' he said. 'Now for the arrows.'

Henry sat watching him and asked.

'Have you done this before?'

'No, not exactly. But before the war, I was a member of the Longbow Society. We held contests all over the country, many times on my estate. Did you know, that for much of England's history, a boy of your age would have to start using the bow from an early age. That was the only way to 'lay your body' to the correct shape. to be a longbowman by the time you were about sixteen? All sport would be cancelled on a Sunday and everyone had to practice archery, by law. Each town and village had its own place of practice where they set up the Butts (targets). In Reading, it was St Marys Butts.

'Wow,' said Henry. 'I didn't know all that. Is that where the name of the street comes from?'

'It sure is. Now, pick up that bow, and with your left arm straight, pull back on the strings with your right hand. You'll need to pull it all the way to your chin if you can.'

Henry tried, and the best he could do was three quarters of the way back.

'Strong, isn't it? Said Maurice. 'I reckon the pull on that is about sixty pounds. Back in the old days, with a bow made by a trained craftsman, a Longbowman would pull about a hundred pounds and an arrow could pierce a foe's armour from a quarter of a mile away. Now, let me show you how to fletch an arrow. I picked up some feathers in the forest; it looked like a fox made a kill here recently. They look just right for the job. Now, using the small blade of your knife; cut a four-inch length of the feather. Then, you need to split that down the middle, as evenly as you can, like so. Can you cut me some more like that please, Henry? I need to see if my glue is ready. I've been boiling up some fish bones from the trout you caught.

'Glue from fish bones, will that work?' Henry asked.

I'm not sure, I haven't tried it before. But it looks a good consistency, so let's hope so. Now, we take one of our cut feathers, a coloured one rather than a white one, and the reason is this.' He pointed to the end of the arrow where he had cut a V-shaped slot and said, 'The bow string fits in that little slot there and we must fix our cock-feather, as it's called, at right angles to it.' Applying a little fish-glue, he stuck the flight to the arrow. 'Now we stick two more feathers, at equal distance apart, on to the arrow. But this time, white ones.'

'Why is that?' Henry asked.

'Because you always load your arrows with the cock-feather pointing away from the bow, at a right angle. That way, you save time sorting out which way to load each arrow. That can be very handy when hunting, or in battle. Time really is of the essence when you have to 'loose' or fire an arrow.'

'But what are you going to do about an arrowhead?'

'Well, we can't do much about that here, but this wood is pretty hard and I think with a sharp point it will be enough to knock down a rabbit or bird. We will find out tomorrow when the glue dries.

On their second day together in the woods, they set off early and were able to stay on their northerly course, without straying too far from the stream. After walking for about six and a half hours, with two short breaks, eating nothing but wild berries, they decided that was enough for the day and that here beside the stream was a good place to camp. Maurice had suggested that Henry stay by the stream with Shep and try to catch more fish, whilst he went hunting in the forest, hoping to catch them some game.

'See you later then.' He called back to Henry, as he walked off into the trees with his longbow strung across his back, and a batch of freshly made arrows in his hand.

'Yeah. See you later Robin!' Henry called after him.

'It was not long before Maurice saw his first choice for supper, in the form of several rabbits hopping about, twenty yards along the trail. He took a deep breath and steady aim on the largest of the bunch then loosed his arrow, whoosh! The big buck rabbit was now supper. As Maurice walked toward the rabbit, he noticed some commotion in the bushes to his right. Quickly as he could, he fitted a fresh arrow to his bow and turned to investigate. It was a young deer, but it had a broken front leg. It was hanging loose from the knee joint. The speeding arrow hit right behind the shoulder and into the heart of the young fawn. It dropped dead on the spot.

'Sorry, young fella.' He said. 'It would have been much worse had I left you to the wolves.'

When he got back to base camp with the supper, he discovered Henry fast asleep on the river bank, snoring softly. Shep was alert as ever and bounded over to meet him.

'I suppose I did push him pretty hard today; we must have covered a good few miles. I'll let him sleep on a while, and get the fire going.'

Thirty minutes or so later, Maurice had skinned and gutted the rabbit, and prepared the deer. Both were beginning to sizzle over the flames, as Henry slept on. But now, his nose was beginning to twitch and he started to talk in his sleep. Maurice was trying to understand what he was saying, so he sat down on the riverbank beside him. As he did so, a light breeze wafted across from the fire and Henry, still asleep, said.

'Cor, that smells nice Aunt Maddie. What's for dinner?'

'It's barbecued venison or rabbit. Whichever you prefer my lord.' Maurice added, joining in.

Henry awoke with a start.

'Oh, I must have dropped off... What's that smell?'

Maurice moved aside and revealed tonight's supper. An hour or so later, all three lay back on the grass, absolutely full. Shep, having eaten the rabbit and then a good deal of venison, was now happily gnawing on a bone. As they lay back relaxing, Maurice said,

'Tell me about Aunt Maddie.'

'How do you know about her?' Henry asked, looking shocked.

'You were talking in your sleep.'

'Oh, was I?'

'Yes. You were asking her what she was cooking for dinner.'

'Well, I don't know why I would be asking Aunt Maddie that. She didn't cook very much at all. We mostly ordered takeaways or heated-up TV dinners, from the freezer. Just pop one in the microwave for two or three minutes, and it's done. No need to wash up either because it's a throw-away dish. Even if it wasn't, we had a dishwasher. Friday nights we would eat out though. There are loads of restaurants in Reading.'

'Really,' said Maurice.

'Yes. Chinese; Indian; Japanese; Thai; Kentucky Fried Chicken; Burger King; and Macdonald's.'

'All those restaurants, in Reading?'

'Yeah, sure. Every pub sells food too.'

'So, tell me this Henry. Is your food better in your other life?'

'Well, to be honest, no it isn't. There's lots more choice of course. But here today, the meat is much more tender and tastier, especially pork. I didn't know meat could taste that good, and fish too. I only really like cod but the fish here is so different. I suppose they don't have to swim in a sea full of plastic.'

'Plastic? What's Plastic?'

'Oh, it's a long story. I'll try to explain it to you tomorrow. I need to get some sleep now, I'm dead tired. Shep's nearly asleep too.'

CHAPTER TWENTY-THREE

As they lay down in the shelter of the trees, Henry could see the stars peering down at them from above and he began to wonder if he would ever sleep in a proper bed again.

They set off at first light. Staying near the stream that conveniently was keeping them on a northerly heading.

'Did you hear thunder last night?' Henry asked.

'I did, but I don't think it was thunder,' Maurice said. 'I think perhaps it was our boys doing a heavy bombing raid on Paris or Caen, perhaps both.'

Henry's mind went back to the time of his school trip, to the war museum. He saw the destruction of the city in giant photographs, and it seemed so strange to think that the destruction was happening right now, with him here to witness it.

'Have you noticed Shep's floppy ear?' Maurice remarked. 'It's erect, like the other one. I wonder why that is?'

'Yes, I'm looking at it now. It usually means he senses danger. Look at the way he's acting, sniffing the ground and running in circles. What is it boy?'

'In that case, we must take great care. Keep your wits about you, we cannot be too careful. Thankfully we still have good cover for the rest of the day. We'll stay on this forest track until tomorrow, but after that we'll have no choice but to break cover. We will face that problem when it comes though, let's push on.'

The rest of the day was uneventful, and Shep had settled down, seemingly less worried now. His floppy ear was back to normal. After finding a good spot to camp, Maurice took his bow and went off to hunt for some supper, leaving Henry and Shep to gather wood for the fire. It was thirty minutes or so before he spotted anything large enough to make a meal. But then, as luck would have it, he heard the gobble-gobble of a wild turkey. The arrow was swift-and-true, and the bird was killed instantly. As Maurice made his way back to camp, he began to pluck the turkey, keeping some of the more suitable feathers for his arrows. When he was nearly back to camp, he could hear Shep making a terrible snarling and groaning noise, and Henry shouting,

'NO, NO!'

Dropping the turkey, Maurice quickly fitted an arrow to his bow and stepped lightly to the edge of the clearing, until he could see what was going on. The scene that met his eyes was horrifying. Shep was enmeshed in a large net that had been thrown over him, and his desperate struggles had made the situation worse. Standing over him was a rough-looking character, with a pistol pointed at Shep's head. Two yards away, another beast had Henry in a headlock, shouting at the man, he had a pistol too.

'Shoot that effin' dog!'

Maurice drew back the string on the powerful bow, as the man's fingers tightened on the trigger.

WHOOSH!

The arrow flew and hit the gunman, right in the top of his arm. Missing the bone, it went straight through and into his chest. But at the same time as the arrow flew, the pistol fired, and the bullet hit Shep in the head. He dropped on the spot.

'You murderer!' Henry yelled. 'You have killed my dog!'

Losing all sense of his own safety, he elbowed his assailant hard in the pit of the stomach. He doubled-up in pain and fell to the ground. Maurice was upon him in an instant, planting a heavy boot upon the man's throat.

'You are Herr Schmidt, I presume. You traitorous dog. How many more men do you have following us? Talk!' He said, pressing down even harder with his boot, watching the scoundrel's face turn blue. 'Talk, tell me how many!'

'Six,' he cried. 'Six more!' ,

'How long before they catch up? Come on, answer me! Damn you.'

Whilst all this was going on, Henry had been trying to release Shep from the net. Free at last, he cradled the lifeless form in his arms. Rocking back and forth, he cried like a baby.

Maurice pulled him gently, but firmly, to his feet.

'Come on boy. I know how hard this is, but there is nothing we can do for Shep now. We have to move. Give me that net and help me get this traitor trussed up.'

Throwing the net over Herr Schmidt, they trussed him up. Ensuring he could not move, they dragged him into the bushes.

Maurice practically had to drag Henry for the first twenty minutes of their escape.

'Come on Henry. We must push on; they are right behind us. Shep was my friend too but it's one of the terrible consequences of war that we have to bear. We all lose friends, even family members, but we must carry on if we are to survive and win. There is no other way I'm afraid, we can't give up, we must stick to our task no matter what. Right now, my task is to get you back home and that's what I intend to do.'

'What's the use?' complained Henry. 'My world has been...'

His words were cut short when they were suddenly confronted by three armed men.

'What do we have here? asked one. 'Looks like Robin Hood and one of his not so merry men'. said another.

'Is that you, Pierre?' asked Maurice, advancing toward the man who seemed to be in charge.

'Well good God, if it's not my English friend, Maurice. You old reprobate, you look like an old tramp. Who is this, who is your sad friend?'

Maurice related the tale of the last few days and also the task ahead of them. Pierre listened intently and at last he spoke,

'Do not worry about the men behind you, my men will take care of them for you, have no fear. But soon you have to leave the cover of the woods and the risk of capture will be much greater. There is a remote farmhouse on your way, where you may sleep. I will draw you a map and send on ahead that you are coming.'

Twenty minutes later, they were on their way again but Henry was still moping about Shep, saying that he didn't care whether he lived or died now,

'What's the point?'

Maurice stopped and turned on Henry,

'Enough, Henry.' His voice was full of emotion. 'Let me tell you something. Those three men we met back there were father and two sons. When the Germans invaded France, Pierre's eldest daughter was raped by a German soldier. Pierre swore to kill the man who had committed the crime but the soldier was protected by the army, so he and his two sons joined the French Resistance. Do you know what the German soldiers did, when they found out? They dragged his wife and two daughters into the village square, and executed them.'

They walked on in silence and it was twenty minutes or so before either of them spoke. In a low tone, Henry was the one to break the silence,

'Sorry Maurice. I didn't mean to be such a burden. It's just that..'

'I understand how you must feel, Henry,' broke in Maurice. 'But we must look after ourselves and concentrate, all the time. If we get caught, I will get shot for a spy, but you will have a worse fate. You will suffer the most horrendous torture, until you tell them all you know, and it seems to me that you know more about Britain's secret plans than anyone.'

'Yes, well. We're still going to win.'

'I hope to God you are right. I can't imagine what life would be like if the Germans ruled Britain. Anyway, let's do our part, stay alert, and get on that boat tomorrow night. In the meantime, I think we will stay in the woods until it's good and dark. Then we can try to make it to the farmhouse. So, first things first, let's go hunting. We are too close to the edge of the woods at the moment, we'd better go deeper in.'

One hour later, the pair were enjoying a spit-roasted fowl of some sort. Neither knew what it was, but both agreed it tasted good.

'Better get a couple of hours sleep if you can, Henry. We may be in for a long night.' But although he closed his eyes, and tried his best to sleep, his mind was once again taken back to that terrible moment when Shep was shot in the head. But at long last, he dropped off.

Back at the scene of the ambush, Shep regained consciousness and slowly opened his eyes. At first, he could not see at all, but as he lay still, his eyesight gradually came back. The first thing he saw, laying right in front of him, was the dead body of the man who had shot him. A few yards away, another body was entangled in the mesh that had trapped him earlier. The sight of the netting filled him with anger, and he tried to spring up but his legs wouldn't let him. He lay still for a few minutes and then tried to rise again. Slowly this time, he unsteadily got to his feet. He looked all around him and then staggered to the stream where he drank and then waded-in, up to his shoulders. Dipping his head under the water several times, he became aware of a searing pain at the top of his skull. He couldn't know this of course, but his executioner's aim, even at such close quarters, was altered by the speeding arrow that hit his arm. Subsequently, the bullet struck Shep a glancing blow, on the top of his head, and had rendered him unconscious.

After ten minutes in the stream, he crawled into the bushes to rest. Instinct told him he was not ready to face the world just yet. Three hours later he crawled out of the bushes and began sniffing around, trying to pick up the scent of his master and friend. It took a few minutes, but he was soon on their trail and despite losing the scent once or twice, he doggedly sniffed around until he picked it up again. After an hour or so, it seemed our two intrepid travellers had met with two, possibly three, other humans. This confused things further for Shep but after much circling around, he was on the right track again. He could tell he was getting closer too. Another ten minutes had passed when he was startled by a gunshot, quite close by. He stopped in his tracks, both ears fully erect. Slowly creeping forward, keeping close to the ground, he peered carefully and quietly through the bushes. What he saw filled him with rage. Maurice had been shot in the arm and now Heir Schmidt was standing over Henry, pointing a pistol at his head.

'Now you will give me the information I want, or you die!' Herr Schmidt screamed.

Springing from the bushes with the speed of lightning, Shep knocked the gunman to the ground. He fastened his fangs around the Germans throat, and didn't let go until Henry's attacker was dead.

Maurice rose from where he had fallen, staggered over, and clearly still in shock, said,

'My God, is that Shep?'

Henry sat on the ground with a blank look on his face and thought to himself 'I must be dreaming. First, they kill my dog, then my friend, and now they are both here. Very much alive.'

Before he could think anymore, Shep was licking his face, in his old familiar way. As Henry hugged and made a fuss of his animal friend, Maurice patted his head. Shep let out an almighty yelp and moved his head away, out of Henry's reach.

'Look Henry,' said Maurice. Look at that bump.'

Shep had a bump on his head the size of a large walnut. As Maurice spoke, blood from his wounded arm dripped onto the ground.

'You're bleeding, Maurice.'

'Yes, but I think it's only a flesh wound. Give me a hand to get this shirt off would you.'

Gently, the shirt was removed and it was as Maurice had thought, a flesh wound. But the bullet was still in his arm. 'First aid kit please Henry. It's in my bag.' Henry watched the big man wince as he poured a generous amount of Iodine over the wound.

'You said to pour it on.'

'Yes, I know. Just bandage it up now please, I'm trying to think what I can use as a sling. Do you have anything in your bag Henry?'

He had a quick look,

Sorry,' he said. 'It doesn't look like I have. But I'll take a look in Schmidt's bag. Hmmm, nothing in here either. Wait, what's this?'

Wrapped in brown paper was a clean shirt.

'This will do, won't it? We can tear it up to make a sling.'

'Yes, that will do nicely, Henry. Hang on a sec though, it looks to be about my size. I'll wear that and make a sling from my old one.'

'Why not? It's beginning to honk a bit anyway.

Well now, yours doesn't smell so sweet either my lad. Help me change will you? It'll be dark enough to move out soon.'

'What are we going to do with him?' Henry nodded his head towards the dead Schmidt.

'Leave him. Let the wolves have him. It's no more than the traitor deserves.'

Twenty minutes later, our three musketeers moved out.

CHAPTER TWENTY-FOUR

They hit the main road sooner than they had anticipated and were pleased to find it deserted.

'Ok,' said Maurice, 'Along here we should find this bridge.' He pointed to the spot on Henry's map. 'Then one kilometre past there, we take a left on to a small country lane, and once we get there the rest should be easy.'

'Listen,' Henry whispered. 'I can hear a car.'

They hurriedly hid themselves in the bushes at the side of the road. Soon, a little old Citroen came rumbling along. The car had hardly any lights on to speak of, the headlights had been blacked out as per the law in war time, with only two thin slits left clear on the glass, just enough to show the minimum of light onto the road. It would seem that the moon would be more of a setback than the car headlights. However, by the time the bridge came in sight, they had successfully avoided detection from the few passing vehicles. The bridge itself was going to be a problem because it had a sentry box on either side, although only one of them seemed to be manned.

'I think I will go ahead and see if I can engage the sentry in conversation,' said Maurice, 'or distract his attention somehow, while you and Shep sneak past.

Keep your heads down until I give the signal. OK. Wish me luck, here I go.' He walked slowly towards the first sentry box and peered in through the glass door and was surprised to find there was a sentry who, was either asleep or dead in his chair, he couldn't tell which.

As quietly as he could, he crept across the bridge to the box on the far side his arm was hurting badly and the pistol that he had hidden in his sling had moved and was now pressing on the bullet wound. He tried to ignore the pain, telling himself over and over that it didn't hurt, but his arm was telling his brain a different story. By now, he had reached the second box and he steeled himself as he walked to the door, still no one challenged him. He carefully peered in through the window, this time there was no doubt as to the sentry's health. He was lying on the floor, in a pool of blood that had come from a bullet wound in his head.

Henry heard the call and saw Maurice waving them over the bridge. They sprinted over to him.

'Looks like our resistance friends have prepared the way for us, thank goodness.' Taking the pistol out of his sling, he said,

'Here Henry, take this will you. It's giving me hell....'

He didn't finish what he was saying because at the sight of the gun, Shep let out a fearful growl and had it not been for Henry's quick thinking and grabbing the dog's collar, things might have turned nasty.

'Down Shep!' he shouted, as he put the weapon inside his shirt. I guess he just does not like guns. Maurice looked quite shocked but as soon as the gun was out of sight, Shep calmed down and his manner towards Maurice became friendly again.

'That's more like it,' said Maurice. 'You are one temperamental dog. Come on, let's move. Our country lane should be up here on the left. Three more vehicles went by, but none stopped. They moved on, and eventually they came to the small lane they were looking for.

'Thank goodness for that,' exclaimed Maurice. 'I need to take a rest pretty soon; my arm is hurting like mad.'

They turned into the lane and carried on along the narrow track that wove its way through fields of two-meter-high sunflowers. No sooner had they turned into the lane when they heard the rumble of tanks and other heavy vehicles coming down the road they had just left. They turned to look. They had a good view of the road from where they were, although they themselves were concealed within the field of sunflowers.

'Good lord, where do you think they are all going with those heavy guns and tanks? Look, there are hundreds of them.' They watched as the never-ending convoy poured over the hill.

'Calais, that's where they are headed. I'll be bound.' Henry said, half to himself, sort of thinking out loud.

'What do you mean, are the Germans going to invade England?' Maurice asked.

'No, it's going to be the other way round Maurice, we are going to do the invading,'

'Good gracious, when?'

'Well. I guess I can tell you. No one is going to overhear us in this field. The first thing is, it won't be for a couple of months yet, and second, our landings will not be at Calais. The allied forces will land all along the Normandy beaches, but the Germans will not be there to meet our troops. They will be waiting with all their heavy armour, this lot I presume,' and he nodded at the convoy. 'Now, when I told Mr Churchill, he thought I was mad. He said *'If we land on the Normandy beaches, Gerry will be able to sink and bomb us out of the water at will. We won't even get ashore.'*

But I told him the Germans wouldn't be there, because they have seen aerial pictures of the massive build-up of an invasion force of tanks; guns; lorries; troop carriers; being mustered, all around the fields and countryside of Folkestone and Dover. They won't have time to get back down the coast to stop our real invasion force from landing. *'Just where do I get such a spare invasion force from?'* Churchill asked. I explained that they didn't need to be real. They could be blow-up dummies and cardboard cut-outs. From the air they would still look like the real thing.

'Will the PM go for it?'

'Yes, the allied commanders went for it and that is what will happen, in a couple of months' time. It will be the biggest invasion force the world has ever known. Incidentally, the place where we are to be picked up tomorrow night, will be code named Utah beach.'

Maurice gave this some thought, then said;

'Utah is American, is it not?'

'Yes, another one is called Omaha. It is because the General in charge of the landings is an American called General Eisenhower.'

'Do you think it's time to move on now?' Said Henry.

They moved on along the little country lane for an hour, both of them deep in thought.

'Let's stop here for a rest,' suggested Henry.

'Good idea, just ten minutes though.'

They sat down on the side of the verge and took a drink from their water bottles.

'How much further do you think? Henry asked.

'About three miles, I reckon.'

'Do you feel ok to carry on?'

'Let me rest Henry, just a while, and I'll be ok.'

Ten minutes later, they started off again, but Maurice was struggling so Henry propped him up. They staggered on, but suddenly Shep stopped.

'What is it boy?' Henry asked, and he noticed Shep's floppy ear was pointing upwards, a sign of danger, and he instinctively felt for the gun tucked in his belt.

Then a horse whinnied, and a voice with a strong country accent said;

'Do you want a lift?'

It was then that Henry saw them, half-hidden by sunflowers, a horse and cart with the driver sitting on a box seat, smoking a very strong French cigarette.

'I've been waiting for you boys, what's wrong with your arm friend?'

'He has been shot,' said Henry.

'Right, let's get him up to the house. Help me get him on the wagon.'

Together, they helped Maurice on to the wagon full of straw. Henry climbed up beside him and told Shep to follow. It didn't take too long to reach the farmhouse where just a very dim light was showing from a front window, as they pulled up outside the front door. They helped Maurice inside.

'Clear that table, Marie.'

A woman wearing an apron, who Henry took to be his wife, did as she was asked. 'Fetch my bag will you please? Oh, and you had better bring some brandy.'

'Are you a Doctor?' Asked Henry.

'No son, I am a vet. Now sit on the table, under the light.' He said, addressing Maurice. 'Let me take a look at that arm.'

Maurice did as he bid, and sat on the edge of the kitchen table. The bag had now arrived, along with the brandy. He reached into his bag and found a pair of scissors, and proceeded to cut the soggy blood-soaked bandage from the wounded arm. Maurice winced as the dressing came away, the wound was red and inflamed. The farmer pushed and pulled at the wound with his fingers, causing Maurice to curse out loud. 'Holy Sh**t!' he exclaimed in English, but the farmer new what he meant.

'Sorry friend, I was trying to find the bullet.'

'And have you?' asked Henry, who had been watching closely.

'Yes, it's lodged up against the bone, and it's got to come out, now.'

He picked up the bottle of brandy and held it up to the light as if to check how much was in it , then handed the bottle to Maurice, saying;

'Here, have some of this. I think you're going to need it.'

Maurice took a swig of the 100% proof old brandy, pulled a face and almost choked.

'Good stuff, eh?' remarked the farmer, as he delved into his bag and pulled out a long pair of tweezers and a very sharp looking knife. 'Take another swig at that brandy my friend, and then lie back on the table.

Maurice did as he was told, but as he was about to hand back the bottle, he changed his mind and took yet another swig.

Then he lay down and said;

'Go on then, let's get on with it.'

The farmer took the bottle and poured a generous amount over the wound; the tweezers; and the knife, before placing the nearly empty bottle on the table, where Maurice could reach it. But before letting go of the bottle, he took a swig himself.

'OK, here we go then.'

Taking his knife, he made a cut across the bullet hole about an inch and a half long. Maurice let out a long yell but to his credit kept his wounded arm still. The farmer looked at him and said;

'Better have another swig before I go in with the tweezers.'

It hurt like hell and it took both the farmer's wife and Henry to keep Maurice still. Shep lay on the floor, and covered his eyes with his paws. Although it was less than a minute before the bullet was finally extracted, it seemed an eternity to all in the room.

'Are you ready for this?' asked the farmer's Wife. She was holding a rather large darning needle threaded with a length of catgut.

'Yes, let's get him sewn up and stop this bleeding.'

The farmer's Wife bandaged the injured arm and helped Maurice off the table and on to a couch. After a final swig of the farmers brandy, Maurice fell into a deep sleep.

'What about you young fellow?' The farmer asked Henry. 'You got any injuries?'

'Thankfully, no.' Said Henry, eyeing up the knife and tweezers on the blood-soaked table. 'Do you think he will be alright?' He asked, looking at the prostrate form of Maurice, laying on the couch.

'I don't know son, but I think so. He sure is one tough Englishman, no doubt about that.'

'Have you ever done anything like this before?' Henry asked.

'Err, no,' said the farmer.

'Yes, he has,' said his Wife. He had to cut off the lower leg of a British airman we had here.

'Oh,' said Henry 'and what happened?'

'He died,' she said, as she cleaned up the table. 'Are you hungry lad?' she enquired.

'Yes, I am.' Henry admitted, as he watched the farmer sink into a chair near Maurice and fall asleep.

'Let's you and I eat then,' she said. 'Those two,' she indicated with a nod of her head, 'can eat when they are sober,' and she handed Henry an oilcloth to cover the table. 'You will find some cutlery in the draw there,' she said.

Nodding with her head towards the dresser, as she put some more logs into the fire box of the stove. She then moved the big old pot over the hot plate and in no time at all, they sat down to a good hot meal of lamb stew and dumplings, with homemade farmhouse bread. Shep was fed from the stew pot too, but mostly meat. Henry sat in an old armchair near to Maurice, Shep lay down at his feet, and the farmer's Wife retired to bed. All was still and quiet, except for the occasional moan from Maurice as he slept. Henry relaxed and tried to sleep, his right arm drooped over the arm of the chair, rested on the back of Shep's head, tiredness overtook him and he too fell asleep.

CHAPTER TWENTY-FIVE

Early the following morning, Henry awoke to find himself sniffing the aroma of fresh coffee. Maurice could smell it too.

'My goodness, that smells good,' he said, half to himself.

'How are you feeling, Maurice?'

'Not so good I'm afraid, my head hurts'

'What about your arm?'

'Oh, well that hurts too, but not as bad as my head.'

The farmer's wife came over from the stove and handed Maurice a large cup of black coffee.

'It's got lots of sugar in it, you are going to need some energy later today. I am cooking ham and eggs for breakfast and you had better eat it. But first, get yourselves over to the barn there.' She pointed out of the kitchen window, 'and get yourselves cleaned up and come back over when you are ready to eat, take these with you.' She handed Henry some clean bandages.

With Henry's shoulder to lean on, Maurice staggered to the barn, where they found not only bales of hay but a water pump that filled a drinking trough. Henry dragged a bale of straw close to the trough for Maurice to sit on and after carefully removing the old bandage; he pumped cold water over the wound that had now stopped bleeding. Together they dabbed the wound dry and applied a nice clean bandage. Half an hour later, after a good wash-and-brush-up they both declared themselves ready for breakfast. The farmer was sitting at the table eating breakfast when the two returned.

'How's the patient this morning?'

'Not so bad,' replied Maurice. 'Your surgery was pretty good considering, but the needle-work, well?' But, to be serious, I must thank you for what you did, you have probably saved my arm.'

'Ah, it was nothing. Now, eat your breakfast before it spoils and afterwards, I will tell you what lies ahead for you both.'

After scoffing ham and eggs like it was their last meal, they were offered more coffee. They sipped in silence and waited for the farmer to speak. After a long while he asked;

'Do you have any money?'

Henry was about to speak when Maurice said;

'Yes. We have a little, why do you ask?'

'I ask, because you have twenty-two kilometres to go before you reach the coast and you my friend, are in no condition to walk.'

'So, what are you suggesting? Maurice asked.

'We could sell you a motorcar, if you could afford it.'

'Well, we can't, and anyway Henry doesn't know how to drive and I wouldn't be able to do it one handed.'

'There's only one solution then. I could lend you my horse and cart. But it will still cost you, because I won't get it back for a week.'

'How much?' Maurice demanded.

The farmer took a pencil and wrote down a figure on a piece of paper and showed it to Maurice.

'Sadly, we don't have that much. We'll just have to walk and that's the end of it.'

'No, wait a minute,' interrupted Henry, 'I have money.' He fumbled about in his haversack and came up with a wad of high denomination notes, and handed them to Maurice.

'Where in the devil's name did you get all this money Henry?'

'It was in the saddle bags of the general's horse I stole, to escape from the chateau.'

So, the deal was done, the farmer produced a rough map and pointed to a country lane that they were to follow.

'It will take you all the way to this little hamlet by the coast, and just here (a little cross marked the spot) is the home of the master boat builder, Monsieur Bouvier. Here you must leave the horse and cart, let the horse drink from the water trough and give him his nosebag.'

'OK so far?' he asked. 'Well, it should be. Jean-Claude knows his way by heart.'

'Who's Jean-Claude?' Asked Henry.

'Why, he's the horse of course. Now pay attention, this is important and you must get it right. Your pick-up time is 0100. You will receive a signal of two short flashes on an Alders lamp. You must respond, only if the coast is clear, by lighting your cigarette lighter three times. Make sense?'

Both of them nodded, but Henry said;

'So, what do we do, just sit at the water's edge and wait?'

'No said the farmer, I'm coming to that now. From the boatbuilders yard, you will have a good view of the beach and there will be many boats moored there, above the high-water mark. Some of them are upside-down having maintenance to the hull, but most are the right way up. What you will be looking for, is a group of boats moored to the left of the beach, that form the letter T, three across the top and four forming the tail. All of them up the right way, except the middle one at the top. That is your boat. It's upside down and it's not big, you will be able to lift it up and crawl underneath. Now, it is an old boat and there are cracks in the planking. You will be able to look out to sea and watch for your signal.

Any questions?'

'Yes,' said Maurice. It is a very long beach, where do we look for the boats forming the letter T?'

'It is the end nearest the boat yard, you will have no trouble finding it.'

The farmer's wife appeared, carrying two pairs of old blue overalls.

'Here, put these on, and you may look a bit more like farm folk. It won't hurt if you both get a bit of cow dung on your boots before you go too. You can rest up in the barn until you are ready to leave. But first, make sure you burn those dirty bandages and anything else of yours you are not taking with you. Go and rest now, we'll have transport ready for this afternoon,' she said, warmly.

On their way back to the barn, Maurice said;

'By the way, do you know how to drive a horse and cart?'

'Yeah, it's easy. You just got to say GIDUP and WOE.'

'What, in English?'

'No silly, in French. The horse's name is JEAN-CLAUDE. Let's get some rest, we should leave at about fourteen hundred.'

The horse and cart were waiting at two o'clock. Maurice climbed aboard and sat on the straw; Henry was going to be the coachman, Shep was happy to walk. They shook hands with the farmer and his wife, and thanked them for their kindness. As Henry shook hands, he passed the farmer four large banknotes;

'Expenses,' he said, 'and our thanks for the wonderful French resistance and all the great work they do.'

With that, he climbed aboard the cart and with a flick of the reins on the horse's backside, they were off.

'Give my regards to Winston Churchill,' called out the farmer.

'Yes, I will,' said Henry. (Little did the farmer know that his regards could well be passed on.)

The map that the farmer had drawn for them was extremely good and they had no trouble finding their way through the narrow country lanes. They were making good time and Maurice had been asleep almost from the start. But now, after about two hours, he was awake and had noticed they'd stopped.

'Everything alright, Henry?' He asked, rising up from the straw. There was no answer, he looked around and Henry had gone, disappeared.

'What in blue blazes is going on here,' he said to himself. Now, what had happened was, they had reached the top of a rather long hill and Henry decided to give the horse a rest for a few minutes, whilst he popped into the woods to pee, leaving the horse contentedly grazing by the roadside. Maurice stood up in the back of the cart and called out 'Henry,' who then appeared from the bushes, doing up his fly.

'What's up?' he cried, and at that moment a black snake about a meter long slithered out from under Jean-Claude's nose who almost jumped out of his skin. This sudden movement caused Maurice to stumble and lose his balance. He toppled forward, trying to steady himself, and clutching at anything to stop him falling. Unfortunately, the thing that came to hand was the lever that released the hand brake. This was enough for the frightened horse and he dashed off down the hill at a terrific gallop, sending Maurice sprawling in the back of the cart. Henry cried out

'STOP' although who to, he didn't know, and started to chase after the runaway horse and cart. Shep too took up the chase, and as fast as he was, he had a job to catch up. When he did, he made an almighty effort to leap on to the back of the cart barely hanging on with his front paws, and then with an enormous heave, his rear legs got a grip and pushed him into the cart. Once on board he could see that Maurice was franticly pulling on the reins with his wounded arm whilst his other hand was pulling on the crude brake lever. But the blocks of wood that served as brake pads were smouldering and were having little effect on slowing the thing down.

As they were nearing the bottom of the hill, with Maurice frantically pulling at the reins, he shouted 'help me pull' to Shep. Somehow seeming to know what was required; Shep immediately took up the reins behind Maurice and began to pull as hard as he could. As they reached the bottom of the hill, and the cart stopped pushing the horse, the combined effort of the handbrake and the two passengers pulling on the reins finally got the horse to pull up and the cart slowly ground to a halt. Twenty minutes passed before Henry caught up with them, almost as tired as the horse.

'Good God,' he panted, trying to get his breath. 'Are you alright?'

'Yes, I think so. Why on earth didn't you wake me?'

'Well, I didn't think you would find the act of me going for a pee in the woods very interesting.' Henry snapped, 'and besides, you looked so peaceful lying there. I didn't have the heart to wake you. How was I supposed to know a snake would spook the horse?'

'A snake, you say?'

'Yes, I saw him slither across the road, a big black thing.'

'Alright, alright. I'm sorry I was sharp with you, but I...'

'It's OK, I know I should have woken you, and I messed up and.....'

'Forget it Henry, honestly. Come on, take hold of the reins will you, my arm is hurting like hell.'

'Oh look, it's been bleeding. Your bandage is soaked. I think we had better...'

Before Henry could finish his suggestion, the sound of a motorbike coming down the hill stopped them in their tracks. As the bike drew nearer, they could tell it was a German army motorbike and side car, carrying two German soldiers. The bike came to a halt a few yards ahead of the still trembling horse. The rider of the bike switched off the engine and dismounted, lifting his goggles from his eyes to his helmet. He walked over to Henry and Maurice; both were still trying to calm the poor horse down.

'What has been going on here?' he demanded in German.

Maurice indicated that he did not know what he said, then proceeded to ask him if he spoke French to which the soldier replied *'nein!'*

'Well, officer.' Maurice continued in French (although he knew the man was a corporal) we were on our way to the coast, when our horse bolted.'

'What's the matter with your arm?' The soldier interrupted, pointing to the blood-soaked bandage.

'My papa fell while cutting the hedge, and a large twig embedded in his arm,' chimed in Henry.'

'Oh dear,' said the corporal. 'Do you want to take a look Doc?' He called to the man in the sidecar. 'He is a medic,' he said, addressing Henry as if to reassure him.

'Is he a doctor?' asked Henry.

'No, he is a medic, it's like a field nurse or something like that, I think.' Maurice said.

The medic came over and he spoke hardly at all, except for 'a-ha' and 'hmm' now and again, as he cut away the blood-soaked bandages from Maurice's arm. His next exclamation was 'Wow!' and turning to the corporal said 'He needs to see a doctor, with all haste, and with that he poured a liberal amount of Iodine over the wound and followed it up with a small piece of white lint and a nice clean bandage. As he was finishing up, the medic picked up his bag, and looking Maurice straight in the eye and in perfect English, said,

'GOOD LUCK.'

With that, they mounted the motor cycle and rode off down the lane.

'Well. What do you make of all that Henry?'

'God only knows. Do you think he was English?'

'Oh no, he was German all right, but I think he knew where we came from.'

'Shall we get going again Maurice? I will walk with the horse, holding his bridle. You jump back up on the cart and we'll plod-on slowly. With luck, we can make the boat yard before dark.'

CHAPTER TWENTY-SIX

It was almost dark when they reached the boat
builder's yard and they were met by a man who
declined to give his name, but did say:

'I have been expecting you. I will take care of the
horse. You must get yourselves into that shed over
there, from there you will be able to see the beach and
the boats and your hiding place. As he was leaving, he
said, 'Good luck, I will go now.' Then he stopped and
said 'one more thing. Each night at twenty-three
hundred hours, the Germans have been posting two
soldiers on all the beaches along the coast. They are
supposed to patrol the whole beach, but they mostly
sit up this end smoking and waiting to be picked up
again.' He took hold of the horse's bridle and led him
slowly out of the yard.

'Better get ourselves into the shed then.' Maurice
observed, and the three of them crept into the dark
shed as the sound of the horse's hooves on the
cobbled street died away. It was dark now, as they had
lost time over the horse bolting, and the medic on the
motorbike who had stopped to help them.

'Do you know, I still think that medic was English'
observed Henry.

'No, I don't think so' Maurice said. 'But I think he
knew we were English and he was a sympathiser.
Perhaps he has some family, or maybe a British

girlfriend. Who can tell? Anyway, we were very lucky, but it has delayed us. I can't see very much of the beach from here, it's too dark and this window is filthy. Henry, will you pop outside and see if you can make out where our hiding place is? Your eyes are better than mine.'

'Yeah, OK. But I think we could do with a bit of help from the moon right now,' Henry said. As quietly as he could, he opened the shed door and peered outside into the darkness. He stepped out, and cursed to himself as he stumbled over something. What it was, he couldn't tell, but it hurt his toe. Moving on around the corner, he came to the window, and just at that moment there was a glimmer of light from the moon as it appeared from behind the cloud. He looked up and could tell it would not last long because another large cloud was scudding along, ready to put the light out. But in the brief time that he had, Henry spotted the upside-down boat at the head of the letter T, as the farmer had described to them. Feeling his way back around to the door, carefully avoiding the obstacle he had previously tripped on, he got himself back into the shed.

'Could you see anything Henry?' asked Maurice.

'Yes, I saw our boat on the beach. It's not far from the water's edge, and I'm sure I can find it in the dark, even if the moon doesn't come out again for us.'

'Good boy Henry, I think we can stay here for another hour yet. But we have got to be careful in case they do put a patrol on the beach. Can you please keep an eye out Henry? My arm hurts like mad and I am going to try to take a nap.'

'Yes of course I will. But don't you think we should go into the village and find a doctor? I'm really worried about you.'

'No, we will not,' Maurice snapped back. 'My orders are to get you back home and that is what I intend to do. Then hopefully I can get to a hospital in good old Blighty.'

'OK Maurice, I' m going to do my best to help you get me home safely.'

'Don't be cheeky now,' laughed Maurice, although it plainly hurt him to do so. He sat down on an old box, leaned back against the wall, and closed his eyes.

'Come on Shep, let's go outside for a quick reconnoitre, and leave the old fella in peace.' Back out in the cold night air, all was very quiet, except for the sound of the waves lapping on the beach. After a few minutes, Henry's eyes seemed to be getting accustomed to the dark and he could see clearly the upside-down boat, where they were to hide, and he could make out the route across the beach to get there.

'Shouldn't be too hard, Shep' he told the dog. 'A piece of cake really. Let's go down to the boat and check it out shall we?' He was looking at Shep as he spoke and the dog's expression seemed to be saying:

'Yeah ok, let's go.'

'Do you know, Shep? I think you understand every word I say.'

It was Shep who detected it first, the faint sound of a diesel engine coming from the far end of the beach. Peering through the darkness, Henry could now make out the faint twin beams of the darkened headlights of a vehicle.

'Let's get ourselves out of sight, Shep' and the two of them crouched behind the dry-stone wall that surrounded the boat yard. The sound of the engine got louder as the vehicle got closer and eventually drew to a halt not fifty feet from where Henry and Shep crouched behind the wall.

'Still' he whispered to Shep, as he gingerly raised his head above the top of the wall and watched as two soldiers jumped down from the back of a lorry, both carrying a rifle. One spoke briefly to the driver in German, which Henry did not understand. The truck moved on, and Henry ducked his head down behind the wall as he listened to the sound of the engine drone away into the night.

Once again, he raised his head above the parapet and the two soldiers were nowhere to be seen.

'Back to the shed Shep' whispered Henry. At that moment, the moon flitted from behind a cloud and the two sentries were illuminated, walking back towards the far end of the beach, from where the lorry had brought them. Henry opened the door of the shed as quietly as he could and was shocked to find himself looking down the barrel of a gun.

'For goodness' sake Maurice, point that thing away from me before Shep tears you to pieces.'

'Sorry' said Maurice. 'I have just woken up. You gave me a start that's all.'

'OK, OK. Now listen,' said Henry. 'I reckon the sentries are going to be gone for at least half an hour, if they are going to walk all the way to the other end of the beach and back again for their pick up. That's if they only do an hour. So I think now might be a good time to get to our boat by the water's edge. What do you think Maurice?'

'Yes, let's go by all means. This place is full of rats.'

The moon once again decided to show, and give enough light to help them along the way. It seemed clear so they silently made their way towards the water's edge and the upturned boat. This turned out to be about two and a half meters long and enough room to hide the three of them underneath.

'Let's see if we can lift it.' Maurice said. The boat was resting on two railway sleepers so there was enough room for them to get their hands under the gunnel, and lift. Henry with two hands and Maurice using his one good arm, the boat was easily tipped on to its side. As it did, three or four little crabs scurried out between their legs.

'Crumbs' muttered Maurice 'it's worse than the shed.' Shep however, thought it was great fun as chasing crabs in the dark was something he had not had the pleasure of before. But Henry told him it was not the time or the place to be playing games. With their backs under the thwarts (seats for the oarsmen) they lowered the boat back down on to the wooden sleepers. As the moon shone now and again, they had a good view of the ocean through the cracks in the warped planking on the boat's side.

At the other end of the beach, the two soldiers sat down on a concrete step and smoked cigarettes. One was a regular soldier, the other a young recruit newly conscripted into the German army.

'And what are we supposed to do if the English come across the sea and invade us tonight? 'Well,' said the older man, 'Do what you were told to do. Point your rifle at them and say,

'Halt! Who goes there, friend or foe?'

'You are joking?" the younger man said.

'Of course I am. If you see an invasion force coming ashore, you do what I do.'

'What's that?'

'Run like hell! But you don't have to worry. The Fuhrer said we have got the British trapped on their little island. along with their American friends. If they try to get off, we will blow them out of the water.' Then he stubbed out his cigarette and said,

'Come on, let's wander back to the other end of the beach.'

This time the two sentries walked slowly back along the water's edge, and when they got to the far end they sat down on an upturned boat. Looking out to sea, they leaned their rifles against the upturned hull and each lit another cigarette.

Inside the boat, Henry and Maurice had heard the footsteps of the approaching sentries crunching in the sand. Henry grabbed Shep and put his hand over his muzzle, to make sure he made no noise as they waited for them to pass. No such luck. They realised they were caught like rats in a trap, with two armed guards sitting on the lid. Henry, for his part, was racking his brain.

'Come on, think. Think! What can we do?' But no answers were forthcoming. However, it was Shep who came to the rescue, well sort of. He passed wind (blew off) loud enough for one of the sentries to hear.

'What did you say?'

'Nothing, I didn't speak.'

'Oh, I thought you .... Mein Gott! What is that rotten smell, Did you......?'

'No, I did not. Don't try to blame me. I'm moving away from you,' and with that he picked up his rifle and his footsteps could be heard crunching in the sand as he walked away. A few seconds later, the second man followed him.

Maurice waited until the footsteps were out of ear shot then he whispered to Henry

'Help me lift the boat, just enough for you to crawl out and take a look-see. Take old stinky with you too.'

Between them, they tipped the boat up until the gap on one side was wide enough for Henry and Shep to slide under, and then drop it down again. Once out, Shep thought now was a good time to have a good old runabout on the beach. 'Stay' whispered Henry, as he peered over the upturned hull, trying to spot the two sentries in the dark. At last, the moon once again was kind enough to show itself for a minute or two and he spotted the two men way up at the back of the beach.

Heavy though it was, Henry was able to lift the boat high enough for Maurice to crawl out. Sitting on the sand behind it, they waited for the sentries to leave. As luck would have it, ten minutes later the German truck returned to collect them. Once again lady luck smiled upon them, because within five minutes of the sentries leaving, an Alders Lamp flashed a signal from a mile out to sea.

CHAPTER TWENTY-SEVEN

The signal had been answered from the beach, using the cigarette lighter, causing Henry to remark,

'I don't see how anybody is going to be able to see that little light; they must be a mile away at least.'

'Don't you worry about that,' Maurice told him 'they can see it alright, in fact you can see a lighted cigarette from fifteen miles away at sea on a clear dark night like tonight.'

A mile off the beach, Able Seaman Boyle spotted the signal from the cigarette lighter. 'Signal from the beach sir,' he called.

'Very good,' the skipper replied, followed by 'Get your dinghy in the water and go pick 'em up.' The strapping seaman jumped into the boat as soon as it hit the water and in no time at all he was rowing steadily towards the beach.

The little boat sat low in the water once it was loaded with three more bodies.

'Right, let's go home then lads,' the seaman remarked, as he took up the oars and put his back into the task.

Meanwhile, the captain had inched his MTB (Motor Torpedo Boat) closer inshore, so that on the return journey, the seaman had little more than a quarter of a mile to row. Once alongside, Maurice was hoisted aboard by block & tackle, on account of his inability to climb a rope ladder with his arm in a sling. With him safely on board, the same method was used to hoist-up Shep. Henry shinned up the rope ladder and was on board, ready to meet Shep on deck. The captain saluted Maurice as he came aboard and informed him that the SBA (Sick Berth Attendant) would take a look at the injured arm and that, all being well, he would be in Gosport's Haslar Hospital within the next couple of hours.

'Now young man,' he said, addressing Henry. 'I'm afraid we can't get your dog below so he will have to stay on deck throughout the crossing. We can chain him up behind the bulkhead here where he will be out of the wind.'

'Well, I shall stay with him sir, if you don't mind.'

'Yes, I thought you might say that. It's up to you, we'll get somethings to try to keep you warm.'

'Dinghy's inboard, sir,' a rating told the captain.

'Right, full ahead both. Let's go home,' was the order, and the powerful twin diesel engines surged into life.

'We are on our way home, Shep,' Henry told the dog, just as a sailor appeared with a straw-filled

mattress for them to sit on and a length of cord for
Shep's lead.

'He looks as though he understands what you are
saying.'

'Well, I'm sure he does,' Henry told him.

'I will bring you a couple of blankets in a minute,
now make a lead from that rope and keep the dog on
it the whole time, skipper's orders. I can get you a hot
drink if you like; coffee; tea; or khi?'

'Khi?' Said Henry 'is that like hot chocolate?'

'Yes, a bit like it, but very thick.'

'Sounds good to me, Shep would like some too if
you can find some sort of a dish to put it in.'

'I will see what I can find for you.'

Five minutes or so later, the man returned with two
steaming mugs of thick hot chocolate and an enamel
dish to pour Shep's drink into. Shortly after that
another sailor appeared with two heavy blankets to
wrap around them, and keep the cold wind off their
backs.

'Glad to see you have got him on the lead,' he
remarked, noticing that Henry had attached the rope
to Shep's collar and wrapped the other end around his
wrist. 'It gets a bit choppy at this speed, so hold on

tight. The SBA gave your companion a pain killer and told him to sleep if he could, but he said he was worried about you two up here in the cold'.

'Tell him not to worry, we are fine and he should get some rest.'

'I'll tell him,' the sailor said, as he disappeared down the hatch. Henry and Shep wrapped themselves in blankets and sipped their hot drinks.

Almost an hour had passed when the skipper appeared on deck, followed closely by Maurice.

'The Major insisted on coming to check on you himself,' the captain said.

'How are you doing Maurice?'

'I'm fine now, thank you Henry. They gave me an injection and the pain has gone. I had a nice tot of navy rum as well.'

'I don't know which of them helped ease the pain better,' the skipper said.

'I know which one I liked best though,' Maurice replied, with a hearty grin.

**

In the early part of the war, a batch of mines had been laid in the waters between England and France. These mines were Contact rather than Magnetic. Big old iron things with horns sticking out. They were anchored to the seabed by a heavy concrete weight, attached by a thin steel rope that held the mine out of sight, just below the surface of the water. When a ship passed over or was close enough to touch one of the horns.......BOOM!

'One of her Majesty's ships is missing,' would be the report. It was the job of Naval Minesweepers to have cleared all the mines from this area. All that is, except this one, and it was armed and dangerous. When it was first laid some three years previously, the cable had got itself fouled up around the concrete sinker, so it did not rise to the surface as it should have. It hovered two feet above the seabed and therefore a danger to no one except a submarine. Now however, the situation had changed. The constant movement of the currents and tides had caused the mine to twist on its short lead and the rusted mooring cable had deteriorated, strand by strand, until all that was left was a single length of wire. This solitary strand, worn down like a thread, was all that was holding the deadly device to the sea bed.

Under the cover of darkness, a Royal Navy MTB had slipped silently out of Portsmouth harbour with orders to pick up two men and a dog from the Normandy coast. The twin engines of the MTB churned up the waters in its wake, and as it raced across the sea it passed over a sunken mine that was straining at its mooring. TWANG!

The last strand snapped and the mine popped up to the surface, some two hundred yards behind the speeding craft, a floating menace, just waiting to be hit. The crew of the MTB were unaware that the wash from their powerful engines had caused the hidden contact mine to be released as they sped across the water on their way to the French coast.

**

Henry and Shep huddled together behind the bulkhead and tried to keep warm. For the first time in days, Henry's thoughts turned to home; Kate; Lady Palmer; the horses; and old Ned the stable lad.

'Wouldn't it be great to go over to Coley and visit George and Mary again...?'

BOOM!

The floating mine hit the boat just below the Port torpedo tubes, blowing the whole boat to pieces in a huge ball of flame. Henry and Shep were blasted high into the night sky turning over and over, tied together by the rope lead.

CHAPTER TWENTY-EIGHT

Henry came back from a black abyss of unconsciousness and slowly he began to be aware of what was going on. He was in water trying to keep afloat then he realised Shep was with him, still tied to his wrist by the rope lead. 'That's why it hurts so much,' he thought. Although he could not fathom out why his hair hurt, or at least his scalp. He would never know it was because each time his head had dipped below the surface, Shep had pulled him back again by his hair. It was still dark but the moon found a break in the clouds now and again. Henry looked about him, they were alone. No boat, no people, nothing. Panic started to set in, 'We have to swim,' he thought. But where to, which way? 'Oh my god, we are done for.'

'Help!' he started to shout, but he knew it was useless, nobody was going to hear. But just then, something gave him a hefty thump on the back. Restricted as he was, with Shep's lead on his wrist, he turned to find they had bumped into a large piece of floating timber, about the size of a railway sleeper. It wasn't wide enough to climb on, but Henry was able to get Shep's front legs over and then he too flung both his arms over and hung on.

Six thirty am, on a lonely beach in Normandy. A fisherman and his wife were preparing to cast their nets, whilst their young son played in the sand. Concentrating on the nets, they did not notice the dog that had appeared, as if from nowhere, and was now tugging at the boy's sleeve.

'Mama, Mama, called the boy. 'This dog wants me to go with him.'

'Well, shush him away,' she called.

'I can't he said, he won't go.'

The mother put down her net, ran up to the dog and tried to shoo him away.

'Go on, shoo,' she said. But there was something in the dog's manner and the way he kept going only a few paces and then returning, that made her think something was wrong.

'Rene,' she called 'there's something wrong here. Come and help me see what it is.'

The fisherman put down his net and said 'oh, what is it now?'

'I don t know, but something is wrong. I'm sure.'

They followed the dog to some large black rocks a mere twenty yards along the beach and there behind them, right by the water's edge, lay Henry. Unconscious, but still alive.

'Quick Rene, go fetch the cart we must get him up to the cottage.'

Gently, the boy was lifted on to a small hand cart. Then the fisherman and his wife struggled to pull the heavy load across the sandy beach to the dirt road that ran across the top. Here, the going became much easier. In less than five minutes they had reached the small group of fisherman's cottages that made up the little hamlet. Henry was taken into the first cottage they came to and was laid down onto a small horsehair couch.

The little group of fisherfolk had no doctor to call on and for years had relied on the old-fashioned remedies dispensed by Madam Ponchard, a ninety-eight-year-old widow-woman who lived at number seven. She always wore black and had a black cat too that seemed to live on her lap. She looked rather like a witch and some would say she was one. Nonetheless she was sent for and twenty minutes later she completed the journey from cottage number seven to number one.

'Mon dieu' she exclaimed 'the boy is dead.'

'No' said the fisherman's wife 'look here, he breathes,' as she held a small mirror close to the boys nose and pointed out the mist that formed on the glass.

'Then get some water into him,' said the old crone. Together, the two women poured a few drops of fresh well-water into the boy's mouth and watched as he licked his lips.

Shep watched and gave a little yelp when he saw the slight movement. Next, the fisherman's wife filled a small beaker from the bucket that had been placed by Henry's bed and held it to the boy's mouth. Instantly his parched and cracked lips began to close on the cup as he sipped, slowly at first, then gradually began to drink.

'Steady' said the old woman. 'Don't let him have too much at first, take it steady. That goes for him too,' as she pointed to Shep who was drinking from the bucket.

'My goodness' the fisherman's wife observed, 'he looks like a Camel stocking up at an oasis, ready to cross the desert.' Gently, between them they pulled the dog away from the water and turned their attention back to Henry. They continued to give him a sip at a time until at last he opened his eyes and with a husky voice said.

'Water, water.'

The fisherman's wife could not speak English but gave him water just the same. As he was drinking Shep stood on his hind legs and licked the boy's face.

'Shep, Shep! Oh boy am I glad to see you,' Henry said, putting his arm around the dog's neck and hugging him like one would a long-lost brother or kin of some sort. 'Where are we Shep, is this England, have we made it?'

'I think the boy speaks Anglais' remarked the older woman.

Realising what he had done, Henry quickly said in French, 'Where am I please, can you tell me where I am?'

'You are in St Pierre Eglise,' the fisherman's wife told him then added 'let me take this cord from around your wrist, it looks so sore and bruised. How do you think the cord got broken?'

'I don't know. I expect the dog chewed it till it broke,' said Henry, then added 'may I have some more water please?'

'Yes, but not too much now. Just take a little at a time, and then try to get some sleep.'

'Thank you both for caring for us' he said as he hugged Shep once again.

'You're welcome. I've seen some strange things come out of the sea hereabouts but never a boy with a dog.

Louis was a freedom fighter and had joined the resistance movement shortly after the German occupation of France. He was a humble fisherman's son but was fiercely patriotic. He was a mere fifteen years old when his country had capitulated. Louis was disgusted that his proud country had surrendered without a fight. 'Well, I'm not having that' he told himself and he vowed to kill as many Germans as he possibly could.

Louis' parents were never told what he did when he left the cottage. They had their suspicions of course but did not question him when he came home, as he did on rare occasions.

'An English boy with a dog you say? Is the dog a German shepherd?'

'Yes, that's right son, and a clever dog he is too.' His father told him how the dog had dragged his mother along the beach to find the boy.

'And is he French, this boy'?

'Oh yes, I'm sure he is. But he speaks English as well.'

'I have a feeling we have met before you know' mused Louis. 'I shall find out when I meet him in the morning.'

Henry was eating some breakfast that the fisherman's wife had brought him and had been told that her son would call in later to say hello.

'He thinks he knows you.'

'Who on earth could that be?' He wondered.

Shep warned Henry someone was coming.

'Ah yes, I thought so. The English boy who speaks French and his dog that understands only English. We meet again."

Henry remembered the day he and Shep had first been dropped into France and Louis was one of the resistance fighters that escorted him through the woods to the bakery to begin his mission.

Louis was eager to know what had happened to Henry since that day and was most interested to hear about Maurice, and his bow and arrow.

'Wow, a real Robin Hood. What happened to him when your boat exploded?'

'I wish I knew' said Henry, with a lump in his throat. 'I wish I knew.'

'OK, I tell you what we had better do. I must leave now but someone will come to fetch you tonight, after dark. We must try once again to get you home. Are you fit to travel?'

'Yes, we have been well looked after by your very kind parents for nearly a week now.'

'Very well my young friend, I must leave now. *Adieu* and good luck.' With that, he left the cottage.

A little after ten thirty, a battered old grey-and-rust-coloured Citroen van rumbled up to the door of the cottage. The driver left the engine running and got out and met Henry at the door. Henry was ready for the off, having said goodbye and thanks to the fisherman and his wife who had retired to bed at their usual time of nine o clock. The driver, a swarthy looking man with long unruly hair, and what looked to be a knife scar from his right eye down to his mouth, opened the passenger door and said gruffly.

'Get in.'

Shep went first. In over the seat and into the back. Henry sat beside the driver. The little van moved on to the beach road heading south, then fifteen minutes later took a left turn on to a small country lane that became narrower and narrower until at last, there was barely enough room for the little van to pass.

'Wow' Henry started to say, but the driver interrupted him and said.

'No speak.'

They moved on in silence, except for the sound of the engine and the bushes scraping the sides of the van. Fifteen minutes went by and they made a right turn, on to a slightly larger lane, and the going got better. A few miles later the van stopped, having pulled off the road and in to a little lay-by..

'Walk now' the driver informed Henry. Making no attempt to get out of the van himself. Henry got out and let Shep out from the back. As he did so he could see the driver pointing up the lane.

'Come on then Shep, looks like we are on our own now.' They walked slowly along the moonlit lane, not knowing how far or where to. But a mere hundred yards was all they had gone before Henry felt Shep had sensed someone nearby and there he was, half-hidden in the bushes. A man in black.

'This way,' he said. 'Follow me.' He turned and led Henry along a woodland path. As they walked, he asked Henry.

'Did you enjoy your ride?'

'You're kidding aren't you?'

'Yeah, talkative fellow isn't he? OK, we're here.' Right there, hidden in the woods, was a log cabin and off to one side was a smaller log building. The sign on the door said PRIVY.

'Follow me,' said the man in black as he headed towards the toilet door at which he stopped and gave what Henry assumed was a signal rat-tat, rat-tat-tat on the door. Seconds later the door opened automatically. 'Come inside and shut the door,' he ordered as he produced a small torch to light up the inside of the small room that was indeed a toilet. Just behind the door was a hole-in-the-ground type porcelain toilet, with two footprints that indicated where to stand, or put your feet. However, the guide was shining his torch on the far wall where he gave another secret knock. This time, heavy bolts could be heard being drawn, followed by the opening of the door. 'This way,' said the guide, and they stepped into a dimly lit tunnel that was sloping down into the ground. Down, down, they went, until they came to another heavy door. This one was open, above the door was the sign:

VIVE LA FRANCE

Shep and Henry stepped through the doorway and were met by the fisherman's son, Louis.

'Welcome to the cavern,' he said, 'come in and meet the boys.'

Henry entered a large underground room that had a big round table in the centre, at which sat seven men and one woman. Most of them smoking foul-smelling strong cigarettes.

'Come in and sit down. Join our discussion,' said one of the older men at the table.

'Have I met you before,' Henry asked?

'Yes, that's right. I was with Louis when you first landed here in France.'

'Oh yes, I remember. You were the one that was going to shoot my dog,'

'Shall we get on?' Said the woman. 'Henry, sit yourself down there.' She pointed to the empty chair next to Louis. 'I will tell you why you are here.' Henry did as he was bid and after a short pause, the woman who was known only as 'J' said 'Henry, you and your dog somehow survived a mid-channel explosion on your boat and got washed up on the beach. Not far from where you started. Is that right? No one else?'

'Yes, right. Just us.'

'Well, it seems there were others. Two men were found drifting in a Carly-float, mid-channel. They were picked up by German patrol boat. The two men, both English, were a Royal navy lieutenant and a man dressed as a farmer.' Henry drew a deep breath.

'So he is alive!' Cried Henry.

'Yes, it looks that way but don't get too excited,' said J. We have been given to understand that they are taking the two men to the Gestapo headquarters, at the château where you were a baker's boy.'

'Oh my God, that's dreadful, can anything be done?'

'Well, we are working on that now. Our spies have told us both men are bound, hand-and-foot, and are being transported in an army lorry. One armed guard rides in the back and another in the front, with the driver. They will be here, at this spot on the forest road,' she pointed to a spot on the map. 'at about six am this morning. Our plan is to fell a tree, blocking the road, to give us a chance to snatch the prisoners if, we are lucky.'

'Where is this ambush spot, can you show me on the map?'

'Yes, it's less than an hour from here so you can rest up for a few hours. If all goes well, you will have a long day tomorrow.'

Henry looked at the map and asked.

'Why did you pick this spot for the ambush?'

'Alright,' said J. 'I will explain. This part of the road is about eight kilometres outside of town and has large trees close to the roadside. One in particular, is a big old oak. If we can drop it across the road as we would like, one German lorry is not going to shift it, and with a ditch on one side of the road and the forest on the other, they can go nowhere. One other advantage we have is that the tree we have chosen is already leaning across the road. We have had men there all day, one of them a Canadian lumberjack, who I have been told can drop a tree on a one-franc piece. But it is important not to drop it too soon, or too late for that matter. However, our armed men will be in the trees, ready to take on the guards and release the two prisoners. By the way, you can ride a horse, can't you?'

'Yes, of course. So can Maurice. But I don t know about LT Baker.'

'Oh, is that the man's name?'

'I assume that's who it is, anyway. Are they both well, do you know?' asked Henry.

'No, we have no information as to the state of their health I'm afraid. We must hope for the best but whatever it is, we must do whatever it takes to stop them falling into the hands of the Gestapo. Whatever it takes, she repeated. There will be no turning back.'

Henry noted the determination in her voice. 'Get some rest young Henry, you are going to need it. Then she added 'Louis, show the boy around, I have things to do.'

'So, what do you think of our Cavern? Asked Louis.

'Yes, I think it's great. Although I have no idea where I am.'

'You're not meant to, that's the idea.'

'How does the air keep fresh down here?'

Louis pointed to a number of round holes in the ceiling. 'Some of those are connected to hollow fence poles around the pig pen but two or three of them are connected to a chimney cunningly hidden in the top of a tall tree. It sucks in fresh air. Over there,' he pointed to a door on the far wall, 'is the little galley. Not much, but we can make coffee and cook a little on a Paraffin stove. Over there, by the gun rack, is the chemical toilet, and that oak barrel is filled with spring water. That little room in there is our bunkhouse, sleeps four in total, but only used in emergencies.'

'Who owns all the guns? Asked Henry.'

'They belong to the men here, real old things some of them, but they all work. Most of them good shots. This door here is our escape route. It takes you out into the woods. We'll go out that way when we leave. Are you armed, Henry?'

'No. I don't carry any weapons.'

'You had better take this then,' and from his shirt he produced a pistol.

Shep who looked as if he was asleep, sprang to his feet and gave a deep throated menacing growl. Had it not been for Henry's steadying hand on his shoulder, the situation could have been critical.

'Put the gun away please, Henry said. 'Shep thought you meant to kill me.'

'The dog looked as if he were about to kill me,' said the startled Louis.

'Oh yes. I'm sure he would have done.'

'Ok have it your way, said Louis, tucking the gun in his waistband. He and three men at the table, who had got to their feet, relaxed a little. 'Alright, panic over,' he said, and they sat down and resumed their conversation.

'Come and join us at the table Henry, J called. Henry sat down with the rest of the men. 'When we leave here,' she continued, 'we want you to go with this man here.' She pointed but gave no name. 'He will lead you to the horses, four of them. Each of you will ride one and lead another to the ambush site. Your route through the forest will take you a lot longer, as we'll go by road. You can leave as soon as you are ready, ok?' Henry indicated he was ready now.

'Well then, let's go,' said his new guide. 'Hold on tight to that animal of yours while I get my gun from the rack.'

Shep made no fuss at all about the gun as they followed the guide out of the door, and into a dimly-lit tunnel that seemed about fifty or sixty meters long. The smoky smell of the cavern had given way to the damp smell of earth, which in turn changed to clean fresh air, as they emerged in the forest. Now they picked their way along a little path to a clearing where four saddled horses were tethered.

'You take those two,' he indicated to two fine looking horses. Henry mounted one and adjusted the stirrups, before setting off.

The first part of the journey was slow-going, through thick bush and thicket. The tall trees blocked out the moonlight but after about half an hour, things cleared out a little.

'Now the going gets easier, can we get a move on,' said the guide.' Do you think you can keep up?'

'You can go as fast as you like, you won't lose us. Shep will always know which way you've gone.'

'Let's go then,' and off he went, setting a very fast pace, considering the terrain. Once or twice, Henry lost contact, but Shep always knew which way they'd gone. Tracking them like a bloodhound.

After an hour's hard riding, the guide slowed the pace a little but still trotted on. Twenty minutes more and they reached a clearing, where the guide dismounted.

'You can get down for a short rest now young man. I must say, you have surprised me with your riding skills, well done. That dog of yours is one hell of a tracker too. Give the horses a drink and we'll move on down that little track.' He pointed to it through the trees. Henry was unable to see it but he was pleased to hear the news. He'd had just about enough of dodging branches and ferns that tried to whip him in the face.

After a short rest, they mounted up and moved into the little lane, it was less than two meters wide and it had deep cartwheel tracks on each side. These however bordered a grassy track down the centre, for the horses. They rode on in comfort with fields and open land on either side. The night was passing and it was beginning to get light. Up ahead was more forest land on their right-hand side. They rode on in silence now with fields on their left and forest on their right. The guide in front held up his right hand, in the manner of a cavalry officer, and the little column came to a halt. Our guide then went on slowly, looking down to his right, at last he seemed to find what he was looking for and beckoned Henry to come on. They left the path and headed once again into the woods. As soon as they were away from the track, the guide stopped and said to Henry.

'Now you must pay attention, we are nearly there. When the job is done, this is your way out. If I am with you then all-well-and-good but if not, you must find your own way. So do your best to memorise the route.'

'OK, I understand.' Henry said. Knowing full-well Shep could find his way back whatever the circumstances. Fifteen minutes later, the guide held up his right hand again indicating they should stop. He turned back to face Henry.

'We are here,' he announced. 'You may dismount, all is calm at the moment.' Henry dismounted and following his guides example, tethered his horses with the other two. 'Come with me,' he said, and lead the way through the bushes, into a little clearing. Straight away, Henry could see the giant oak with a V shaped wedge cut into its trunk, about a metre from the ground. From where he stood, Henry could clearly see the road along which his good friend Maurice and the naval officer would be travelling as 'prisoners'.

'They will be here in approximately thirty minutes,' Henry was informed. 'We have a motorcyclist riding ahead of them and he will spread some tin tacks and nails on the road out there, in case our tree fails to stop the lorry. So, you Henry, must keep the horses in readiness for a quick getaway.'

'Motorbike coming,' yelled a voice from down the road. 'Get that tree down, swing those axes.' The woodman's axe sounded loud and clear in the early morning air, followed in no time at all by an almighty crash as the giant oak that had stood there for more than a hundred years, came crashing down onto the road.

'Back to the horses, Henry,' said the guide. 'We must keep them calm when the shooting starts. We can't have them panicking and bolting. Quick now, here comes the army truck.' They turned and hurried back to the horses that were waiting in the little clearing, twenty metres from the road. Henry untied the reins of his horses, and held them ready for a quick getaway.

'Come here, Shep,' he said 'and sit.'

They waited like this, in silence, but the gunfire didn't come… Henry and the guide exchanged glances but all the man did was shrug his shoulders as if to say 'I don't know.' Suddenly, Shep was on his feet, as two men emerged from the bushes.

'My God!' Exclaimed Maurice. 'I thought you were dead, and Shep too. How did you do it? How did you escape from that terrible explosion, and how come…..?' He seemed lost for words but threw his arms around the boy as though he was his long-lost son. Just then, Louis appeared from the bushes.

'So, this is your Robin Hood then' he said to Henry. ,

'Yes, that's right.' Henry said.

The guide who had waited quietly through all this said 'OK, let's get mounted up. We must get a move on, it's getting far too light for my liking. Can you ride a horse, sailor?'

'Well, yes I can,' said LT Baker. 'It's been some time, but I'll soon get used to it again.'

'Good. Get yourself up on that horse, and let's get out of here, back to the Cavern.'

The four horsemen picked their way through the forest, on their way hopefully to freedom. At the stream they had crossed earlier that morning, they stopped for a short break to water the horses and both Henry and the guide were eager to know why there was no shooting at the rescue.

'Well, I must say your resistance boys really had it planned to a tee,' said Maurice. The driver of the lorry and the armed guard in the cab could see at a glance the game was up. When they screeched to a halt just yards from the fallen tree and saw six or seven masked men pointing guns at them, they climbed down from the cab with their hands in the air, calling for the guard in the back to do the same. They surrendered without a shot being fired, and hardly a word spoken. The three Germans were left sitting in the road, in front of the fallen oak tree. Bound hand-and-foot.

'Well, that's a great result for all of us,' said the guide. 'Let's mount up and move on.

Back at the Cavern, the rescue team were already back and celebrating a successful mission with a glass of good French wine, standing to raise a glass as the rescued captives arrived. They too were offered wine,

Henry had fruit juice. Maurice was talking to two of the men that he had met before while LT Baker tried to make out what they were saying. He didn't speak any French, but from the tone of the conversation he gathered that something important was going on. Henry was also listening, and he began to look worried.

'What is it?' asked Baker.

Maurice turned and said 'I will explain. It seems for some weeks now signals have been coming in, indicating the Germans have been building a new weapon. It's reported to be a new kind of long-range rocket, containing a completely new type of explosive. The explosive is apparently so powerful that if fired into England, it will do more damage than all the bombs dropped on London, to date.'

'Wow,' said Baker. 'That's some weapon. How big is it, do we know?'

'It is reported to be about 30 meters long. It is being built in an underground factory two kilometres south of Aramas, look here on this map.'

He looked up and his French companion nodded,

'So it will travel along this route to its launching sight at Calais, meaning it will have to cross this bridge at Arras. That's where it could be stopped.' He said, tapping the map. 'A team of your commandos has arrived to assist our boys with blowing the bridge, and there is a very large haystack in the field nearby which they will set alight, to guide the bombers of the RAF to their target. They are on stand-by at the moment in Kent, so the plan is to blow the bridge as the rocket approaches by which time your RAF boys will be in the air crossing the channel.'

'Well, that all sounds very well planned, how can we help?'

'You can't get involved at all,' said J. 'We have strict instructions from London. Dependant on the success of our rescue mission to escort you to this spot here.' Again, she pointed to the map. 'Here we are to hand you over to another group of our lads and they are going to get you safely into neutral Spain ASAP. So, you are not to get involved with the rocket at all, but on behalf of my fellow freedom fighters and myself, I thank you for the way you are risking your lives for my country, and for freedom. That goes for you too, sailor.' Although he did not speak French,

He understood the word *Merci*. She hugged and kissed them all on both cheeks and said 'now, you should get some rest. You move out again in a few hours, and you will take the same horses you came on. LT Baker made no comment, but Henry watched as he massaged his buttocks with both hands and his mind went back to the time he first tried to ride Trouble, and had to stuff a cushion down inside his pants.

Later that day, the four horsemen set out again, followed closely by the ever-faithful Shep. Two hours later, as they came to the edge of the forest, they stopped for a short break high on a ridge that looked out over a beautiful valley. As they gazed down, their guide told them 'This is where the rocket is expected to appear, somewhere along that valley road, and there is the bridge where it will be stopped.' The light was beginning to fade now and Henry's eyes scanned the valley for signs of life or movement. It was then that he saw it, smoke coming from the top of a giant haystack, and in no time at all, it was fully ablaze.

'My God. Would you look at the size of that thing,' Maurice exclaimed.

Then, on the horizon, Henry spotted what they had been waiting for. Spitfires, Hurricanes and Lancaster heavy bombers were making their way towards the target, guided by the enormous beacon. Henry and Maurice looked on, as first the bombs obliterated the bridge. Realising it was now impassable, the convoy had stopped and was frantically trying to turn around. But the road was too narrow. The British had now started to drop flare bombs, bright illuminating flares that dropped slowly to earth, hanging on little parachutes. Soon the target was bathed in light. The Germans manned their guns and switched on their search lights, looking for the British bombers. From his vantage point a few kilometres away, Henry sat on the high grassy hill, with one protective arm around Shep.

Watching as the bombers dived one after another, dropping a cluster of bombs at low-level. The Germans latest secret weapon took a direct hit, and what followed was the largest recorded man-made explosion, and everything within 20 kilometres was blown to kingdom come.

EPILOGUE

The rain stopped and Madeleine went out to the front gate and looked anxiously down the road,

'He should be home by now' she thought, 'I do hope he is alright after that thunderstorm, where can he be?' Just as she was about to go and search for him, Henry came around the corner. 'Oh thank goodness,' She said out loud as she watched an 11-year-old boy in a very wet Man Utd shirt trudge slowly towards her. 'Henry' she cried out, 'Where have you been, and why is your phone turned off? I have been so worried.' Henry ran up to her and said,

'I think I was struck by lightning Aunt Maddie, I've had the strangest experience, but I can't remember anything about it now.'

'Oh my goodness said Madeleine, do you hurt anywhere?'

'No, I'm alright now.'

She gave him a big hug and said,

'You're soaking, take off those wet clothes and get into a hot bath, give me your mobile phone and I will see if it needs charging. Oh, by the way. Your girlfriend called to say she would pop round about six thirty to show you her new dog. I think it was the girl called Kate with the blonde ponytail.

Henry was indignant.

'She's not my girlfriend, she's just a friend.'

'Well, whatever. But hurry up, she will be here in half an hour.'

Henry came downstairs in time to see Kate coming through the garden gate with a beautiful Alsatian dog, his left ear was a bit floppy and his tail bent over a little to the left, but a beautiful looking dog nonetheless. Henry went out to meet them and bent down to stroke the dog. As he did so, it licked his face.

'I think he likes you,' said Kate.

'What have you called him?' Asked Henry.

'Well, what do you think Henry? I've called him Shep..........'

Printed in Great Britain
by Amazon